AN EYE ON THE WHIPLASH AND OTHER STORIES

Henry Murphy lives in Sandymount with Mary and their children. He is a practising barrister. This is his first book.

An Eye on the Whiplash
and other stories

HENRY MURPHY

ASHFIELD
Press

This book was typeset by
Gough Typesetting Services for
ASHFIELD PRESS
an imprint of
Blackhall Publishing,
26 Eustace Street, Dublin 2.
(e-mail: blackhall@tinet.ie)

A catalogue record for this book is
available from the British Library.

ISBN 1 901658 10 4 pb
ISBN 1 901658 11 2 hb

This book of short stories is a work of fiction. The names, characters, cases
and incidents portrayed are entirely the product of the author's imagination.
They do not, nor are they intended to, resemble any person, living or dead,
or any actual case or incident. Any perceived resemblance is coincidental.

Printed in Ireland by
Betaprint Ltd.

FOR MY MOTHER
AND IN MEMORY OF MY FATHER

Contents

Acknowledgments

I owe a deep debt of gratitude to many people.

Not so long ago, I nervously passed what you are about to read to the publisher, Gerard O'Connor. Instead of returning it to me, he elected to pick it up and run with it. I thank him for his courage.

I appreciate the considerable expertise of Carole Devaney in the task of editing the text.

I am extremely grateful for the assistance I have received at various times from Doreen Callan, Marie Kelly and Nivés Collins.

Colin, Jenny, Stephen, Declan, Eoghan and Cillian were vital literary consultants.

No words of mine can do justice to my wife Mary for her contribution.

There are many more. In particular, I would like to thank those family and friends to whom I showed these stories. Without their encouragement, I would not have gone ahead.

To each and every one of you, my thanks.

Henry Murphy

September 1997

The Claims Manager's Daughter

Two years in the Library and my first full Brief. Oh yes, I had been in Court for my Master during my devilling year and had made minor applications on my own behalf in the interim. But not a real Brief. Of my own.

My father had warned me before I came into the Library. Many times he had warned me. Not to expect too much too soon. It would take time, he had said. More than once. He himself would have liked to have done the Bar, but his father couldn't afford it and encouraged him into banking instead, starting as a cashier in a dull suburban branch before rising, with caution and a good deal of age, to the vertigo-inducing heights of Assistant Manager. A barrister-manqué, he had envied as much as encouraged my progress through College and the King's Inns.

He had always put five years on it whenever I tried to pin him down. But from my vantage (or perhaps more accurately, disadvantage) point, with two years done in the Library, I wondered if this was not an estimate that bordered on the negligent. On this particular morning, there was nothing to suggest that in three years time I would be able to stand up and announce to all the world, 'I have a practice'. On every day for two years – or more precisely, every day for two years on which the Law Library was open, thereby allowing for weekends and generous holidays, called Vacations – I had meticulously checked my pigeon-hole for post, and precious little post there had been during that period, if one excludes the reminders for my Law Library subscription. But perhaps a turning point had been reached.

I took my time opening the large brown envelope that had 'Dermot McNamara, BL' printed proudly on it. It could not have been printed more proudly had I done the job myself. I looked around in the hope that my moment was not going unnoticed. I was not disappointed.

Re: *DPP v. Barbara Wilkinson*

Dear Mr. McNamara,

I act on behalf of Ms. Wilkinson in the above-entitled matter which comes before the Court on the 9th inst. My client's father would like you to appear on behalf of his daughter.

Accordingly, I am writing to you to enquire if you are available on that date. Kindly revert as soon as possible.

If you are available, I would suggest a detailed consultation at 9.25 on the morning of the hearing.

Yours sincerely,

J. Arnold O'Reilly

Was I available on 'the 9th inst.'? It wasn't necessary, but I checked my diary. Out of self-respect. I was available every day for the rest of my life, for God's sake. As my correspondent well knew.

I pencilled in the case for the 9th and went for coffee.

You will have noted the suggestion for a 'detailed consultation at 9.25'. As our relationship developed, I discovered a number of gentle eccentricities about my first solicitor, J. Arnold O'Reilly. One was that he always requested a 'detailed' consultation. I was never to discover the difference between a 'detailed' consultation and one that was not 'detailed'. Another was that the rendezvous was always for an oblique time – 9.25 or 9.55, for example, never 9.30 or 10.00 like the rest of his colleagues. But then, he was not like the rest of his colleagues. More of this at a later date. For the moment, the un-expected excitement of my first Brief and the delayed commencement of a career.

* * *

One week to go. In the timeless tradition of the Bar, there wasn't a colleague that I didn't pester in the run-up to the great day. Not a book on the topic that I didn't read and re-read. I would have dearly liked a consultation in advance of the 9th, but my friends advised me that the consultation was normally held on the morning of the case and that to interfere with that timetable might suggest to my solicitor that I was not capable of taking the case in my stride or, even worse perhaps, that it was my first outing.

I did not sleep the night before. I arrived in the Library with pages of notes and submissions, every question for examination-in-chief and cross-examination written out, every other word highlighted or underlined in red, yellow flags marking every page.

The word was out. Contemporaries wished me luck. Most had already been through the experience of their first Brief. A small few only vicariously. Not having much to do in those early days, we tended to follow one another around – a sort of rent-a-legal-crowd, a mutual support group. But also, if the truth be told, to witness the possibility of the matador being gored. Library folklore has it that, on the occasion of another first Brief, the budding El Cordobes, appearing on behalf of a defendant before a particularly nasty piece of judicial goods in particularly malign mood, rose to his trembling feet to conduct the first cross-examination of his career, only to find, on so rising, that despite his best efforts he was unable to emit anything even remotely approaching a sound. In a word, he had choked. A protracted silence gave way to beady embarrassment and the flight of the aspiring matador, last seen wigging his flowing way in the direction of O'Connell Bridge.

And so, at 9.25 on the dot, on this red letter day in May, bewigged and gowned, I moved centrestage at last, responding with enthusiasm and elegance to the call of my name. Could anyone have missed my name being called? I made my way downstairs and towards the main entrance to the Library. (My seat is some distance from the main display area of the Library in what is affectionately called 'the crèche', the main display area being reserved for more established barristers.) My journey in law to date flashed before my eyes – the boredom of law lectures, all those dinners in the King's Inns dimly remembered, the excitement of starting off in the Library and the frustration of waiting for work, all of this culminating in my first cap this morning. At last, the first rung of the ladder. Behind me forever the empty bag and the empty pigeon-hole.

As I strode, with nervous authority, out of the nest that is the Law Library into the big badness of the real world, where I would be truly on my own, I wondered if any of those established colleagues noticed.

* * *

Let me interrupt this narrative to confide in you how this precious Brief winged its noble way into my pigeon-hole. You will, of course, have heard it said that 'contacts' are very important in the Law. I would just like to confirm this insight and this Brief as its illustration. It is not that merit and ability may not have a part to play on a later day in the context of what could be called 'Brief retention'. But as to whether merit had a role in the winning of this Brief, it most certainly did not.

A few years ago, my father was Captain of the local golf club and during his tenure a good friend of his, Mr. Wilkinson, who happened to be the Claims Manager of a prominent insurance company, was elected a member of the same club, much to the chagrin of more meritorious candidates. That word merit again. Lo and behold, when the Claims Manager's daughter gets into a spot of bother, who does he turn to only the former Captain's son, with the unspoken promise of 'more where that came from' in the event of a favourable result being achieved.

So much for how I became involved. What about J. Arnold O'Reilly of J. Arnold O'Reilly & Company, Solicitors, of 203 Gardiner Street? How did he come to be instructed by Mr. Wilkinson? Further, how did he come to be on the panel of solicitors retained by Mr. Wilkinson's insurance company to handle their very lucrative personal injuries work? Obviously, this is information which I acquired further down the journey of our relationship, but I think it as well that you be in on the secret at this stage. In pride of place on Mr. O'Reilly's mantelpiece is a black and white photograph showing himself scoring the winning try for Deansgrange RFC in the final of the East Leinster League, the Deansgrange team captained on the occasion by Mr. Wilkinson, later Claims Manager.

* * *

Mr. O'Reilly's office is on the third floor of a building in Gardiner Street. The hall door, like so many centre city offices, opens directly onto the footpath. At 5.30 in the evening, it is not altogether clear if the public assembled outside No. 203 is queuing for Mr. O'Reilly or for the bus home. Little more than twelve hours later, Mr. O'Reilly is to be seen clearing the footpath outside his front door of all nocturnal artistry. (Not exactly Fitzwilliam Square, the geography of which would be more familiar to Mr. Wilkinson and his staff.) It is an old-fashioned building and gets more old-fashioned the higher up you go. Mr. O'Reilly is in no rush to update or modernise. There is a smart brass letterbox in the door, a large one intended to take delivery of the substantial envelopes that are part and parcel of a solicitor's post, but never big enough, I was later to discover, for the one I happened to be delivering in the early hours of the morning.

Closing the door, you leave behind the sounds and smells of the throbbing city and enter a sort of time warp, a placeless sort of place. You might wonder if you will meet anyone ever again. A narrow staircase with a wooden handrail rises before you. A gloomy climb to the first floor. There is no going back. The staircase is not in the occupation of any of the tenants and so is neglected. The only light comes from above the door. The first floor is occupied by what is euphemistically called a gymnasium, the second by the headquarters of the Communist Party of Ireland (of which Mr. O'Reilly is most emphatically not a member) and the third, closest to heaven, by Mr. O'Reilly's less than state-of-the-art offices. All this on top of the flagship that is the 24-hour fast-food joint on the ground floor. Next door is a sex shop called ' ice & Naughty' [sic], while across the road is a Chinese take-away called 'Goodview Restaurant', a somewhat flattering assessment of the architecture of Mr. O'Reilly's building.

I have a feeling that the old rugby captain, now Claims Manager, does not make it very often across the river to No. 203 Gardiner Street.

And so to J. Arnold O'Reilly.

'You must call me Arnold!' Mr. O'Reilly insisted on our first meeting. It was one of the transitional difficulties starting at the Bar, learning to call colleagues and solicitors many years your senior by their first names. It was particularly awkward when you had already known them for many years as 'Mr. and Mrs. So and So'.

Arnold was a big man. In all directions. An enlargement of his former self. It was difficult now to identify the formidable centre three-quarter of the early sixties, noted as much for his acceleration past his opposite number as for his bone-crushing tackle. A reputation that, looking at him now, you had to take on trust, for evidence there was not.

If he no longer looked an athlete, his physical presence was still impressive. Which is more than could be said for his intellectual presence. Unfortunately, most of his endowments had been channelled into his body rather than his mind, with the result that his mental application came as something of a disappointment.

He looked his fifty-something years. I am not sure where 'seed' is, geographically speaking, but Arnold had definitely gone there – and back. Whether it was all those bone-crushing tackles or all the years above the fast-food joint in Gardiner Street, I cannot say.

He had long, heavy eyelids that seemed most reluctant to open and when they did, they revealed large, round eyes that looked at you most vacantly and in a manner which suggested that understanding was some distance behind. Over the years he had shed most of his hair, but what remained was cared for like the Book of Kells. Coal black, each strand was sprayed with great love and affection at more than regular intervals. He was a likely candidate for a wig, but that might have been just a little obvious and I admired him for resisting the temptation – that is, of course, if it existed other than in my imagination.

Altogether, therefore, Arnold achieved a certain balance between physical presence and intellectual absence. It being my first case and Arnold being a solicitor so much my senior in age and experience, I was for a time at least in a certain awe of him and accordingly the portrait I have just drawn was one that was assembled over a number of years. Not all of it was apparent on our first meeting, not consciously anyhow.

* * *

Accordingly, back at the Library, my name called, I advanced towards the door with military precision in the fervent hope that my wig and gown would conceal from Arnold and Client my twenty-three years and corresponding inexperience, while at the same time confer a certain gravitas.

'Gravitas' – the very word. Only a few weeks earlier, I had had a conversation about this word with a colleague some years my senior. We were whiling away a few hours before coffee break, pondering the qualities that make a barrister great. We decided in the wisdom of our inexperience that it is all a question of perception. An image. Confidence and authority. If you portray greatness, greatness will be bestowed upon you. A conclusion to be put to the test the very next day by my colleague.

With Olympian stride he entered the consultation room, filled with important witnesses. Brief and books held ostentatiously to his pompous breast. With a sweep of his flowing gown he seated himself and, as he did so, a button from his waistcoat popped and within seconds solicitor and important witnesses were on their knees searching under the table for Counsel's button. At our post-mortem, we decided that there must be a little more to greatness and gravitas than we had yet to offer.

I should have mentioned to you what *DPP v. Barbara Wilkinson* was all about before starting the consultation. Ms. Wilkinson was charged with dangerous driving, more particularly that on 5th August last she had driven a motor vehicle (the summons specified the registration number of the car, which is not of much interest to you but was silent as to the fact that the car in question was her father's convertible Saab) upon the public road at or near White's Cross in a manner dangerous to the public and contrary to the Road Traffic Act, 1961, as amended.

My very first consultation and we had a consultation room too. No lying up against the wall in the square hall outside the Library for Mr. Wilkinson et fille. This was a significant case. Armed with my Brief, which lacked only the once-mandatory pink ribbon, and the relevant statutes, I led Ms. Wilkinson's legal team into the consultation room and the introductions.

No-one had prepared me for Ms. Wilkinson. Up to this moment she was but a client, without face or for that matter body. Leggy and lovely, she took me and my trembling hand by surprise. I recovered just in time to greet her parents and her curiously unremarkable boyfriend, who had been in the car with her at the time.

Any one of these ingredients would have been enough for a fledgling barrister to contend with – one's first Brief, the prize of inclusion on an insurance panel, the sophisticated beauty of Ms. Wilkinson – but all three together were overwhelming. I could only pray that my knocking knees went unheard.

I probed into every corner of the case in meticulous detail. Truly, not a stone unturned. I was determined that no moment of that fateful evening would be kept from me. Much of my interrogation must have appeared intrusive, voyeuristic even. Despite my best efforts, the relevant instructions were very limited.

Client and boyfriend had had a few drinks (not too many, I was assured) in Temple Bar and were going for a spin in the old man's car before dropping boyfriend off at his apartment in Eglington Road. All they could tell me was that as they drove along the Bray Road at about two in the morning, a ban-garda stepped out at the last moment, almost causing them to crash, and flashed them down. They did not then, and still do not, know why she did so. They were brought to the police station where, fortunately, Client had the presence of mind to insist on her own GP being called to carry out the sobriety test. This perhaps explains there being no prosecution for drunken driving.

Ms. Wilkinson, as fresh and seductive as the summer night on which these things came to pass, gave her account to me in a most sincere manner and, of course, I swallowed every word.

I was at a loss to explain to Mr. Wilkinson why the prosecution had been brought in the first place. Obsequiously, I agreed that it was outrageous and joined in the family indignation at how their daughter was being treated. Mustering confidence, I assured all and sundry that before the morning was out, the prosecution would be successfully routed and the entire sorry chapter deleted from the family history.

There was nothing further to be discussed apropos the case and so, with twenty minutes to kill, we repaired to the public restaurant. I don't know if you have ever been in this particular establishment, but I assure you that it is the noisiest, chattiest, liveliest place in town. Life's rich tapestry all in one room.

Packed, in the pre-Court rush, with barristers and solicitors and apprehensive clients. Animated conversations. Last-minute instructions. Soothing coffees. Wigs and gowns, books and papers strewn over chairs and tables. Later in the day, results would come through. The room would ebb and flow with winners and losers. Hopefully, in a short while, it would hum with the report of Ms. Wilkinson, brilliantly acquitted of driving her father's convertible Saab in a manner dangerous to the public.

I was in no mood for concentrating on the coffee or the lighthearted conversation that accompanied it. Seated in my wig and gown, I interrupted their flow frequently to confirm some fact that had been confirmed umpteen times before. Clients and witnesses did not always appreciate the complexity of the enquiry. If I wasn't checking a detail with Ms. Wilkinson or her boyfriend, I was retracing my copious notes. I was too engrossed in these last-minute preparations to note the stir caused by my client at adjoining tables.

★ ★ ★

Almost 10.30 and time to head over to the Bridewell. A few cases were heard before ours which, with hindsight, was unfortunate. One such involved the spectacular acquittal, on entirely technical grounds, of a driver many times over the limit. This stunning success was achieved by the very senior Junior, Donal Dowling, BL, a specialist in drunken driving cases.

Judge O'Mara was furious. He knew the Defendant was over the limit. The whole Court knew. And yet he had to listen to the careful, relentless reasoning of Donal Dowling explaining how the chain of evidence had been broken. Eventually he had to accede to Donal's application for an acquittal. In that moment, I wasn't to know the extent of the shadow that Donal's win would cast over my efforts.

DPP v. Wilkinson was called and I rose to my proud feet.

'I appear on behalf of the Defendant, My Lord, instructed by J. Arnold O'Reilly & Company,' I announced to the Court, my first words in the pursuit of justice.

I was so impressed by everything that had been said at the consultation that my confidence was such that I was wondering smugly if the State would proceed with the case. Such was my conceit that I was rather hoping that they would, notwithstanding the obvious lack of evidence, so that rent-a-crowd would witness a win brilliantly carved out by me on the merits rather than by default.

The case commenced. To say that the State evidence took me by surprise would be something of an understatement. I struggled to disguise this surprise. The evidence unfolded via a relay of Gardaí who pursued Ms. Wilkinson over half the city and county. During the pursuit, it quickly became obvious that red lights held no terror for the young motorist, her inclination was to favour the continental tradition of driving on the right side of the white line, and keeping within the speed limit had all the excitement of a Vatican Encyclical on sexual morality. At the moment of climax, it was reported that our heroine was doing 100 mph when hailed by the flashing ban-garda.

Wave-like, my moment of glory was receding just as soon as it arrived. I was conscious of a packed Court. Rent-a-crowd carefully tuned to every word.

'Well, Mr. McNamara? Do you wish to ask this witness any questions?' enquired His Lordship.

Unfortunately, no questions sprang to mind. I was completely taken aback by the evidence that was being adduced and how different it was from the instructions that I had received. There was a lengthy pause while I did my utmost to think of something to ask. Eventually, 'No, My Lord,' I replied to a surprised Judge and an even more surprised solicitor. I wondered what questions might conceivably have occurred to my attorney in the face of this evidential onslaught. As if he heard my thought, a pad of indecipherable notes was placed frantically beneath my nose. I was going to have to do better. Why hadn't they told me some of this, I thought to myself?

One Garda witness after another.

'Any questions, Mr. McNamara?'

Arnold was surprised that I didn't have any questions. I was surprised. All that homework. All those questions prepared into the early hours for every possible line of cross-examination. To no avail. Silence. I was beginning to panic. Suddenly the Court was becoming very hot. What would portly Donal Dowling, BL, have asked the Gardai?

'Mr. McNamara?'

'My Lord?'

'Perhaps this witness?'

'Are you sure?' was the only question to come to mind. A titter sprinted around the Court.

'Sure of what, Mr. McNamara?' enquired the Judge.

I fumbled at my notes. I could nearly name those of my erstwhile friends who were enjoying my discomfiture.

'Are you sure, Garda, that the evidence you have been giving is the truth, the whole truth and nothing but the truth?'

'Perfectly sure, Mr. McNamara. Perfectly sure,' replied the Garda sympathetically.

I sat down. I had this vision of Ms. Wilkinson crossing her endless legs around countless briefs from her father's company. The case was running away from me faster than her convertible Saab.

The final incontrovertible straw in the evidence was when Client's GP arrived footless at the Garda Station to pronounce on her state of sobriety. The Gardai saw their chance to at last even up with this doctor who was always finding his patients sober. They followed him out to his car for the purpose of arrest, just in time to see him clamber into a taxi with just the hint of a two-fingered gesture from behind the misted window as the cab sped off.

The State's case ended at last.

To call Ms. Wilkinson or not? Spur-of-the-moment decision. Not possible to seek advice. I was on my own. Like never before.

I had very few options. I could put her into the witness box or I could keep her out of it and rely on some of my finely prepared submissions. Or I could run out of Court and maybe become an Assistant Bank Manager.

It was this last option that was preoccupying me when His Lordship patiently enquired, for the second time, 'Will you be going into evidence, Mr. McNamara?'

I was on the point of telling him that I didn't know when I realised that this was for real, no mere moot, and I couldn't give an answer like that.

'If your Lordship would bear with me for a moment?'

From the manner in which Arnold was leaning his full corpus on the table between us, in an attempt to communicate with me, and at the same time pointing in the direction of the Client, I gathered that he was of the view that Ms. Wilkinson should be called. Unfortunately, I had had a bad cold on the day of the lecture about 'The Realist School of Jurisprudence' and therefore missed the advice that when you have a good-looking female witness and a male judge, get her into the witness box as soon as possible.

From what little I knew of the criminal side of things (and this was, after all, a criminal prosecution – well, sort of), the golden rule was at all times and in all cases and at all costs to keep the client out of the box. It seemed to me that this was the route to go in this case.

Her recollection was rather skimpy and she really had nothing to offer in the face of the comprehensive Garda evidence. Lamb to the slaughter.

My mind was made up. Ms. Wilkinson was not going into the witness box.

'I will not be going into evidence, My Lord,' I announced before an astonished solicitor. 'But I would like to address Your Lordship.'

'Certainly, Mr. McNamara. Will your submissions take long?'

I thought that what was called for was a sharp, concise submission along the lines of the one composed by me around three that morning. But could I find the page?

'No, My Lord. I will be very brief and to the point.' I did not expect to be quite as brief as I turned out to be.

Fumbling with my notes, an embarrassed silence descended on the Court, emphasizing my fingering of the papers before me. By now I was becoming quite uncomfortable and realised that it was touch and go as to whether or not there would be any submission at all. Pages that had been filled with enlightened writing just a few minutes ago suddenly were devoid of script, blank as the mind that sought to read them.

His Lordship came to my assistance. 'Mr. McNamara, I am sure that what you have in mind is that notwithstanding the Garda evidence, the State has to prove its case beyond a reasonable doubt.'

'Precisely, My Lord.'

'And that I should have a reasonable doubt in this case in view of the fact that no accident occurred and how can the driving be regarded as dangerous in the absence of a crash.'

'Precisely, My Lord.'

'And that while the Defendant may not be entitled to get off scot-free, at least she should get the benefit of the doubt and the charge should be reduced to careless driving.'

'Precisely, My Lord,' I repeated, mantra-like, as I sought to invest my emasculated contribution with a little dignity.

'Thank you, Mr. McNamara.'

* * *

Life would later teach me that very often one's mistakes would not reach the light of day but would sink without trace or, at least, where they were destined to taunt one they would not do so until a reasonable cooling-off period had elapsed, so that one was not required in the same moment to handle the mistake and its publication.

This lesson was for another day. It had no application before Judge O'Mara, who had no hesitation in identifying the mistake and holding it aloft, Host-like, for all to see. Each nail in the Defendant's coffin was a nail in my career.

Judgment was succinct and unsparing. It consisted of a savage attack on my client and did not neglect her passenger and family.

'One of the worst cases of dangerous driving I have come across in my twenty years on the Bench . . . arguably the most dangerous stretch of roadway in the country . . . attempted murder of the ban-garda . . . wouldn't even get into the witness box to explain her conduct . . . while she is not charged with drunken driving, I cannot ignore the facts that this may be the reality of the case . . . parents not without blame . . . allowing their irresponsible offspring the use of high-powered vehicles in the middle of the night . . .' was about as much as I could catch of the joyless judgment.

'No doubt. Lucky to get away with the maximum sentence. Disqualification, two years.'

His Lordship leapt off the Bench in a manner akin to the ban-garda's escape from the path of the convertible Saab.

I gathered up my papers, and my future, and headed out of Court with a sinking feeling. This was not the result I had envisaged.

An empty corridor. The Wilkinsons had gone. Without as much as a word. To his credit, Arnold sought to console me with some hollow words. But the bare corridor said it all, confirmed my suspicion that this was something short of my finest hour.

To this day, I have known no lonelier moment. All that prepara-tion. Such expectation so mercilessly dashed. At least if they had given me a hint of the reality, I might have had some idea as to how to deal with the Garda evidence. Instead, all that injured innocence and 'My daughter wouldn't do anything wrong'. They might have hung around for a moment anyway, to shake hands and say 'You did your best'. Perhaps even, 'We made a mistake. We should have come clean with you instead of telling you a pack of lies'.

'I am sure it was not as bad as you say,' my friend proffered over coffee in a quiet corner of the restaurant later in the day. 'Worse,' I replied. 'I am sure you asked a few questions?' he added, trying to put me together again. 'Not a single question throughout the entire case,' I said, determined not to be patched up.

'And what submissions did you make?' 'Not a single submission. The Judge made them for me. It was awful.'

My friend, seeing the hopelessness of the task, gave up, muttering something about putting it down to experience.

* * *

An ominous silence descended on the case for a number of days. Eventually broken by Arnold's phone call, intimating what I already knew, namely that Client et père were unhappy with the handling of the case. Why hadn't I cross-examined the Gardai? Hadn't I heard of the Heavy Gang and the Birmingham Six? The appalling vista? Why hadn't I called herself to give evidence? They wanted to appeal, bring in Senior Counsel and hold a consultation. Any residual hope I harboured that perhaps I was a little harsh in my self-assessment was blown out of the water by this phone call. They wouldn't even trust me with the Appeal. I was crestfallen.

Then I heard that David Richards (DR to his friends) was the nominated Senior Counsel. I was mortified. There were many Seniors who would not be too conspicuous leading me in such an Appeal. But Richards – he was straight out of the top drawer, the very personification, in both physical and intellectual terms, of the majesty of the law, a brilliant all-rounder whose particular speciality was constitutional cases. He wouldn't have done a Road Traffic District Court Appeal in twenty years. How would I explain this very public humiliation to rent-a-crowd? My insurance future was looking decidedly less assured.

At least at the consultation to decide the future of *DPP v. Wilkinson* (and indeed mine), Richards had the loyalty to opine that from what he had been told of the District Court débâcle there was no chance of appealing conviction successfully and precious little chance of softening the sentence. In the latter context, he thought that the Defendant herself might be the trump card. Not for her evidence, but for herself, you understand. She enjoyed the flattery, ignoring the blatant sexism of the tactic. My assessment of the situation was not sought. In fact, my silent presence went unnoticed. However, I have to say that DR helped my withering reputation as best he could. He knew the District Judge from old and was able to inform us as to his penchant for Gardai and prejudice against fast drivers. He had practised in front of this judge in forgotten days on Circuit and one of the latter's endearing little habits was to send down a note of reprimand, while the Court was sitting, to any barrister who might have had the suicidal audacity to overtake him on the road to the town where the Court was sitting.

As I left the consultation, I heard the Claims Manager enquire the name of the portly barrister who had the drunken driver acquitted. But out of the corner of my eye, I caught DR shaking his head sagely and that was that. Good for DR.

* * *

My departure from the Library on the morning of the Appeal was as sheepish as it had been ostentatious on the day of the District Court. I had said nothing to my pals but, sure enough, as I entered Court 3, there they were – rent-a-crowd, every unoccupied one of them, loyal to the last bead of my embarrassment.

Up went DR to the front bench, causing quite a stir by his entry. Arnold in front of him. I was entitled to sit next to him because the Circuit Court is Junior Counsel's Court. But in the circumstances, I contented myself by tucking in behind the great man.

I forgot to tell you that it was decided at consultation not to appeal conviction. This decision was influenced by the form of the usual incumbent of Circuit Court 3 whose prejudices bore a stark resemblance to those of the Court below. I should confide in you, not to be passed on to the client, that I was not exactly committed to the success of this Appeal. The only way any small honour might be salvaged on my behalf would be if the Circuit Court affirmed the District. Any improvement in the Client's situation was a further nail in my coffin. Accordingly, the usual incumbent of Court 3 suited my disloyal purpose perfectly.

I was sitting in my bench before it dawned on me that there had been a change of judicial presence. Subbed up at the last moment. I suspected foul play. Judge Walsh, fixer-extraordinaire and Lothario to boot. How lucky and unlucky in one.

Judge Walsh took one look at the leading constitutional lawyer, by coincidence a former devil, and we all knew where things were heading. Any semblance of anonymity for me was gone when the Judge interrupted to say, 'I see Mr. Richards in Court. You are most welcome, Mr. Richards. Can I do anything for you?'

'That is very kind of you, My Lord. I am in the second last Appeal with Mr. McNamara. Sentence only. Won't take very long.'

'I'll take it immediately,' responded the Judge.

'I am very grateful to Your Lordship as I have something in the Supreme at eleven o'clock.'

As DR launched into an eloquent recital of the facts, I received a thumbs-up from one of my colleagues, not known for his discretion or sensitivity. It would be any Junior's dream to be led by DR, but not in a Road Traffic District Court Appeal.

Back to Judge Walsh. He summed up the situation instantly. Important client. More accurately, gorgeous daughter of important client. Important case for solicitor. Bad result for Junior at threshold of career. Client went to trouble and expense of engaging top-flight Senior. Form of District Judge known to Judge Walsh. Notorious for going over the top. In any event, the two had had a falling out some years ago. Must do what he could to restore the status quo.

'Mr. Richards, I hear what you say on sentence and I am sympathetic, but what about conviction? Was there any evidence of dangerous driving?' enquired His Lordship disingenuously.

I could hardly believe my ears. I had to restrain myself from jumping to my feet and shouting out about the traffic lights and the centre white line and the speed and the footless doctor.

'Well, My Lord, there may have been some evidence of speeding. Perhaps I should call my client?'

'A very good idea, Mr. Richards.'

The trump card.

The business of the Court came to a standstill as the trump card made her voluptuous way to the witness box. She crossed her endless legs as she settled in, the only movement that the purring Judge missed in her entire performance, in no way due to any lack of attention on his part. Straight from 'The Gate'. She never took her eye off His Lordship as she gave her evidence. She spoke softly. He inclined towards her. With every wilting word, sentence was reduced and conviction looked more vulnerable. The packed Court nodded silent belief to every pretty utterance of her restored recollection.

When she concluded her evidence, the helpful Sergeant sought to assist the Court by pointing out that the evidence in the Court below was to the effect that an entire police station had chased the heroine halfway around the counties of Wicklow and Dublin at grand prix speeds before a brave ban-garda put her life in the hands of the Defendant in an attempt to hint to our Formula One superstar that the race was over.

This evidence would have been of enormous assistance to His Lordship (and to me, hence my encouragement of the Sergeant) had he heard it. But as soon as the helpful Sergeant rose to his solid feet to deliver himself of this exocet, Judge Walsh said, 'I will not need to hear further from you, Sergeant. I am satisfied having heard the evidence of the very plausible Ms. Wilkinson that I must have a reasonable doubt in all the circumstances as to the question of dangerous driving and, accordingly, I dismiss the charge.'

I could not believe my ears.

'I am grateful to Your Lordship,' concluded the great DR. He hardly heard Judge Walsh wish him 'Good luck in the Supreme' as he swept out of Court in a manner fitting into the ecstatic embrace of the entire Wilkinson family.

I decided that I had no role in this celebration and muttering some lie about being on my feet in another Court, which went unheard in any event, I slunk off down the stairs. As I did, I heard Arnold telling Mr. Wilkinson, Claims Manager of an insurance company for which I almost did some work, that he never had any doubt about the outcome after the introduction of David Richards, SC.

★ ★ ★

2

An Excess of Alcohol all around

For two weeks before Christmas, young William Dunne, heretofore unemployed, worked selling Christmas trees from a large field, the former football home of Shamrock Rovers. It was hard work, from nine in the cold morning until about eleven at night, chopping and carrying, until, it seemed, a tree had been sold to every home in Dublin. There was no great intimacy between William and work. Indeed, he confided in me later, he felt much more relaxed since he gave it up. Work, he observed, was greatly overrated. However, the money was good and he would earn enough to pay for Christmas.

Built like a jockey, his capacity for alcohol belied his diminutive appearance and his youth. He had arranged to meet a few of his buddies in his local on St. Stephen's Day when they held their annual pilgrimage, which consisted of a pub crawl around some of the capital's better-known watering holes. The journey began in Ryan's, where William cashed in his gift tokens. Down river on the far side to the Brazen Head, on to Mulligan's, northwards to Mooney's, finally resting in Nelson's off O'Connell Street.

Most of the serious drinking was done in Nelson's. Countless pints, the odd ball of malt, the odder sandwich. At the end of the procession, it would be easier to calculate the consumption of alcohol in gallons rather than in pints. Towards closing time, William called a round in celebration of his birthday the following day. As his friends rose to toast him, William went in the opposite direction. He had passed out from drink. His friends went with him by ambulance to Jervis Street Hospital, where he was detained for three days with alcoholic poisoning. It was a few weeks before he was over the incident and had recovered his confidence sufficiently to resume his favourite pastime, the consumption of alcohol. However, subsequently he developed breathing problems, diagnosed as asthma. As far as he was concerned, he had never had breathing problems prior to the incident on 26th December.

Almost three years to the day after this sorry episode, William was in his local, sipping his unearned pint, when he read in the evening paper about a fellow being awarded £5,000 damages for finding a toothbrush (someone else's) in his bottle of Guinness. The finder had alleged that his cancer was due to the toothbrush. The report sparked a chain of thought in young William's mind which, converted into action the very next day, found him joining the queue outside No. 203 Gardiner Street, professional home of J. Arnold O'Reilly & Company, Solicitors.

'Mr. O'Reilly's the man,' whispered William's favourite barman conspiratorially. 'Did a great job for me when I had me accident.' As good as if the President herself had given the nomination. William lost no time.

'You were nearly barred,' Mr. O'Reilly informed William the next day, delivering an early blow to William's confidence in his new advisor.

'What could he possibly mean?' thought William, knowing only too painfully that he had indeed been barred – for a full year, no remission – from Nelson's.

'Statute-barred,' clarified Mr. O'Reilly, picking up William's confusion.

'Oh, I see,' said William, little the wiser.

Mr. O'Reilly took illegible instructions which he passed on to unconscionable Counsel who set the whole daft ball rolling by means of a Civil Bill. William was claiming £30,000 against the hostelry for personal injuries for negligence. If you read the details of personal injuries set out in the Civil Bill, you would be forgiven for thinking that the barrister had mixed up his cases.

Apparently, William had suffered 'great shock, discomfort and insomnia'. In addition, 'his entire way of life had been adversely interfered with. His domestic, sporting, recreational and' – wait for it – 'working lives had been devastated'. It was unlikely he would ever make a full recovery. The asthma was pleaded, of course, and for the sake of completeness, post-traumatic stress disorder. 'He suffered mood swings and was irritable at home. He had difficulty with concentration. This was only occasionally.' (Presumably 'occasionally' because he was not called upon to concentrate very often.) 'He didn't go out as often as he used. He suffered low self-esteem.' And the pièce de résistance – 'He didn't enjoy a pint as much since the incident.'

The allegations of negligence were set out in alphabetical order and in such a way that would suggest that either the Judge did not understand English or was retarded, or both:

A. Failed to take any or any adequate precautions for the Plaintiff's safety;

B. Failed to be aware at all material times of the Plaintiff's presence on the Defendant's premises;

C. Failed to warn patrons and, in particular, the Plaintiff, of the dangers of coming on the Defendant's premises and, in particular, the dangers, well-known to the Defendant, of consuming too much alcohol thereon;

D. Caused and/or permitted the Plaintiff to consume an excessive quantity of alcohol;

E. Sold an excessive amount of alcohol to the Plaintiff;

F. Failed to refuse to serve alcohol to the Plaintiff;

G. Failed to enquire of the Plaintiff at regular intervals as to whether or not he was consuming too much alcohol;

H. Continued to serve alcohol to the Plaintiff notwithstanding that he was at first speechless and then footless.

And so it went on and tautologically on, until the English language surrendered. At all times failing to address the fundamental allegation, namely:

ZZ. Failed to spoon-feed the Plaintiff.

As time passed, William had managed to convince himself that he had been made to consume the alcohol under duress. So when Mr. O'Reilly informed him of the publican's allegation that he was guilty of contributory negligence (stated bluntly by the pub lawyer, 'drinking too much'), the bold William, past whose creamy teeth an even creamier pint only rarely ran (or so he claimed), went berserk and wondered loudly if he had to put up with such abuse and, momentarily forgetting Mr. O'Reilly's calling in life, threatened to see a solicitor about suing to protect his reputation.

There is a breed of Counsel who, when the chicken comes home to roost, is adept at the tactical withdrawal — in lawyer's terms, the hand-over; in layman's, the hospital pass. The author of this Civil Bill never intended tarnishing his reputation by standing over the contents thereof in Court and hence Arnold O'Reilly's urgent phone call to me at 4.25pm, just as I was leaving the Library for the day. I lied that I had to consult my diary and, having encountered the blank page, lied again that I could probably juggle a few things around. In truth, after the débâcle of *DPP v. Wilkinson*, I was surprised to receive the phone call at all and privately rejoiced at the opportunity to re-ingratiate myself with Arnold, who would have to be accommodated — probably for the rest of my life.

* * *

I had a lot on my plate for the evening without Mr. Dunne's problems. I was organising the Circuit Dinner in honour of my Master, who had at last taken Silk. I had been prompting this move since the end of my devilling year. The Circuit Judge was attending and, being the Junior on the Circuit, I was deputed to attend to his every, mainly alcoholic, need. In addition, there were one or two other matters of which more anon.

I decided to forget about Mr. Dunne's problems until after the dinner. I would watch my own drinking and get home about midnight to make up the Brief.

The Circuit Dinner was going well. Too well. Champagne to start with, followed by an excellent Australian Chardonnay. The great refectory of the King's Inns, which had hosted innumerable students' dinners, buzzed with the prattle and anecdote of the members of the Circuit. Without the supervision of the Benchers, reserved for students' nights, the evening, fanned by the two fires on either side of this most exclusive dining room, unwound more quickly. Senior and Junior, male and female, met and mingled, casting off the uniform of the day-to-day. Briefs briefly forgotten, the silent exchanges of the working hours were given substance as time stood still. Even the Judges on the walls began to mellow.

For once the meal rose to the occasion. At dinner's end, snuff and a decanter of vintage port was brought to each table. Uniquely, the Judge had managed to stay awake and deliver a witty speech. I felt that my duties had been discharged. Conscious of my Brief, I had my eye on the clock, but also on the beautiful Afric at a neighbouring table. The clock hadn't a chance.

The Library was unanimous as to her beauty and divided only on the matter of whether or not her slightly generous thighs were a plus or a minus. Many a coffee was devoted to this topic. There was no mistaking the side of the fence on which I resided.

She had come into the Library the year after me. Why the Library I have no idea. As far as I was concerned, if she had auditioned for 'Pretty Woman', Julia Roberts would never have been heard of. Unfortunately, if we happened to be in the same company, I choked. Only once was I on my own with her and that was over coffee in the Barristers' Restaurant. I don't think she noticed me pouring the sugar into the ashtray.

Tonight would be different, I assured myself. About midnight, we were disgorged from the colonial splendour of the King's Inns into its moonlit garden, from where I made my optimistic way to Leeson Street. There was little room in the disco and even less around Afric. She spent the rest of the evening surrounded by a host of ageing, balding, paunchy Seniors, briefly relieved, or so it seemed, of their sleeping responsibilities in Foxrock and Killiney. Afric did not mind the attention; indeed she seemed to revel in it and was, of course, blissfully unaware of me. I decided to finish up my £15 bottle of plonk and retire.

It was about three in the morning as I made my way footless along the canal, the scenic route to my rented accommodation in Clanbrassil Street. By now, my emotions were a pot-pourri. Dinner had been a success, my pursuit of Afric didn't even get out of the starting blocks, I was drunk and Mr. Dunne's Brief was beginning to establish itself in my unconscious. This was one of those 'if only' moments – if only I had plucked up the courage, if only I had gone straight home after the Inns, if only . . .

I was too far gone to read the Brief this side of what would have to pass for a night's sleep. I set the alarm for 6.30.

* * *

I had long envied my colleagues the manner in which their Briefs were prepared. Maybe the pink ribbon was a thing of the past, but at least typed statements and some semblance of sequence, if not a Case to Counsel, an index and the Brief subdivided into separate books as appropriate. Not the solicitor's original file, handwritten statements and attendances (illegible), original vouchers and not a typewriter in sight. Have you ever tried to read Arnold's attendances with a hangover? After two hours' sleep? I was not yet very experienced and liked to prepare my case thoroughly, which involved writing out relevant questions for examination-in-chief and cross-examination. (This was a tip I had received from the Chief Justice. Not personally, exactly, but I had heard that that was how he liked to make up the Brief. Though I doubt if he would have quite as many pages or questions.) Anyway, I read enough to realise that William Dunne and I had a certain orientation in common.

As usual, Arnold had a 'detailed' consultation arranged for 9.25. Unfortunately, I could not be there: firstly, because I was late and, secondly, because of a Motion which I had forgotten in another Court. Between one thing and another, no 'detailed', nor indeed any, consultation took place. Considering the result in the Wilkinson case, where we did have a 'detailed' consultation (at least insofar as the Client's instructions permitted), perhaps the absence of a consultation might be no bad thing.

The one aspect that I was absolutely clear about was that this case had to settle. The case could not and must not be allowed to go on. Firstly, because I was so hung over I was incapable of running a case that particular morning and, less importantly, because it was a complete bummer of a case. 'In a word,' I told a less than entranced Solicitor and Client, 'it is unstateable. We will be laughed out of Court.' I think they suspected my real motive. I was having a hard time laying the ground for a settlement.

If it was an uphill battle so far, it became a veritable Everest when I discovered that Oliver Cummins was on the other side. Nobody had ever settled a case with Oliver. He prided himself on battle and if ever his insurance company client, from whom he was inseparable, was showing any sign of weakness, Oliver would step into the breach with the necessary word of bellicosity.

'Not even you, McNamara, could hold out much hope for this

one' – Oliver's opening salvo. I so wanted to agree with him, cut out the bravado and go back to bed. I had to mutter something about a publican having a duty of care to people who came on his premises to get plastered. Oliver assured me that he would do what he could (which, of course, was untrue), returning quickly to say that he had been instructed that the best his client could do was to bear his own costs to avoid the publicity. Out of a curiously contradictory combination of cowardice and conviction, I did my level best to persuade first Arnold and then William of the prudence of this course. Arnold responded by saying that since the Client was not a mark, he had nothing to lose by running it (and, of course, this was true), adding that he would not charge William if the result was unfavourable. How benevolent.

I was getting about as close to settling this case as I was to the lovely Afric some hours before.

'No, Arnold, the Call-over is not in Court 6; it is in Court 10 where it always is for Circuit Court cases and always has been for as long as you have been in practice.' (Or so I'm told.) Another charming idiosyncrasy of Arnold's: notwithstanding all his years of coming down to the Four Courts for cases, Court procedure always came as a great surprise to him.

As luck would have it, who bounced onto the Bench, looking as if he had been in bed at 10.00pm with a cup of drinking chocolate, only our bacchanalian Judge from the night before.

* * *

Dunne v. Nelson was called. I looked despairingly at my opposite number for any flicker of brinkmanship or the possibility of a settlement. Neither. I would have done anything. Made a contribution myself. Anything. Hopeless. Arnold was writing furiously even before I had begun to say anything. I struggled to open the case, opting for brevity. Early judicial intervention was not encouraging. It was difficult to know whether a Judge who espoused alcohol or abstinence would be best for this case. No doubt anyway about which we had got.

I called the Plaintiff. By now I was in an appalling state. Every one of Anthony Gormley's 40,000 terracotta figures pounded around in my head, sweat ran freely throughout my body, neither rhyme nor reason to my questions, irretrievably lost. I was in the late stages of a panic attack, experiencing an uncontrollable urge to run out of the Courtroom.

Somewhere in the distance, I could hear the Judge say, 'You have already asked that question, Mr. McNamara. Do you have any other questions?' How was the Judge so on top of things? I had not prayed for years, but I surely prayed now – not for success, but quite simply that I would stay awake for the remainder of the case.

It dragged on interminably. I had got to the stage that if it did not end very shortly, I would be asleep. Is it possible to fall asleep on your feet in the middle of asking a question, I pondered? Arnold kept passing me his illegible notes which were of no assistance for the conduct of the case, but at least served to rouse me momentarily.

Remotely, as if in another Court, I heard His Lordship ask for Mr. Dunne's date of birth. I sensed a significant moment, though the significance escaped me. The Courtroom went quiet. There are turning points in cases and I felt we had reached one here. Arnold fed me the answer.

It transpired that the birthday William was celebrating in advance was his eighteenth and accordingly, declared the Judge, 'All the drinking took place while Mr. Dunne was an infant in law, which has a bearing on the Defendant's duty of care towards the Plaintiff. Of course, if Mr. Dunne had been of full age, he would have no case, but being an infant, the Defendant failed in the duty which he owed to Mr. Dunne, firstly in permitting under-age drinking and, secondly in failing to ensure that the Plaintiff was not served an excess of alcohol, bearing in mind his tender years. In all the circumstances, I do not find contributory negligence. I do not think that this episode and the Plaintiff's asthma are related. I award the Plaintiff £5,000 and costs.'

Oh wise and noble Judge! It was all I could do to restrain myself from rising to my feet and applauding. The fug was clearing imperceptibly. I could just make out the dismay on the face of my opponent. Up to a moment ago, it had all been one way. When you have done everything in your power to settle a case and have been met with a stonewall of smugness and meanness, there is no greater satisfaction than, as you leave Court, hearing your opposite number explain the word 'Appeal' to his uncomprehending client.

Outside, a jubilant Mr. Dunne with Arnold telling him that the result was never in doubt. No room for me. Warmed by the hope that some at least of the damage wrought by *DPP v. Wilkinson* might have been repaired, I went home to bed.

* * *

3

Messiah

Not only Arnold's consultations were off the hour or the half-hour. So were his phone calls. Around 6.25 most evenings. It could be any time between 6.25 and 10.25, but mostly 6.25, or maybe 6.35. Always after hours. Never during the working day. Never in the Law Library. Arnold was a bachelor, you see, and, having devoted most of the day to administration, he would catch up on his files for a few hours in the evening. And every file meant a phone call to Counsel. Not for Arnold the convenient and conventional letter seeking your advice, which might earn you a modest fee. Oh no. For Arnold, direct and immediate contact and no fee. Queries which any self-respecting apprentice would have known the answer to or which, indeed, I had given him the answer to on several previous occasions. Not for Arnold to fill his mind with these learned titbits when a tea-time phone call will resolve the matter just as quickly.

Anyway, back to the phone call. I was by now about six years in the Law Library and had taken the premature steps of getting married to a colleague and having children (as luck would have it, twins) long before I was able to afford either. At 6.25 in the evening, I am not long in from a hard day drinking undrinkable coffee 'on the taxi rank' and am helping my wife with two dribbling, badly-needing-a-change-of-nappy babies – what is euphemistically called 'quality time with the kids'. Meals to be eaten, domestics to be attended to, briefs to be read, dictation to be done – 'promises to keep and miles to go before I sleep'. And, of course, inevitably, Arnold's phone call.

The routine is familiar by now. 'Is that you, Dermot?' (Who else?) 'Do we need an up-to-date medical report in *Murray v. O'Neill?*'

Now Arnold has the advantage over me. He has been reading *Murray v. O'Neill* for the past hour and a half or perhaps day and a half. I haven't seen the papers in *Murray v. O'Neill* for perhaps six months. I have no idea what the case is about and certainly do not know if we need an up-to-date medical report, which in any event is a question well within Arnold's, or should I say any solicitor's, competence. It doesn't occur to Arnold that I might have a bottle in one hand and a nappy in the other, and when I reply that I may not quite have all the salient facts of *Murray v. O'Neill* at my fingertips just at that moment, Arnold mutters surprise and I am made to feel that somehow I may not be up to the job.

'Perhaps, Arnold, if you were to read me out the previous medical report?'

Extraordinarily, he does not have that before him. He does not say 'Hold on'. He simply puts the phone down. I hear footsteps. Opening of cabinets, shuffling of papers, muffled conversations and then, inexplicably, taped music. Not Pachelbel's 'Canon' or some similar soothing delight which wafts one off so that when one is eventually reconnected after a symphony or two, one has utterly forgotten the purpose of the phone call. No. Arnold's taped music is 'Three Blind Mice, Three Blind Mice, See how they run . . .' and other minor classics. On more than one occasion, I have screamed at his secretary not to put me through to the music, but to no avail.

Arnold returns, exultant. Apparently we have an up-to-date medical report and he puts down the phone. No apology, no gratitude, no 'au revoir', no fee. Until the following evening then – at 6.25.

* * *

This particular evening is a little more promising or so it would at first appear.

'How are you fixed for the morning?' asks Arnold.

A leading question that no barrister, however inexperienced, should answer in the affirmative until he knows what for. It is usually the prelude to some appalling hospital pass – a right-of-way case or a building contract. Two days at least. More than likely no money in it or else why pass it over at the eleventh hour?

I actually have a messy Application, but I may be able to pass it on to some unsuspecting colleague. I want to keep Arnold sweet. We have been together now for a few years. I have been doing quite a bit of his last-minute work. I never seem to be his first choice. I am

Arnold's '6.25' team, the 'C' team. The run-up the ladder was proving neither as rapid nor as smooth as I had anticipated. Arnold's practice was not the summit of my ambition, but for the moment there was no other summit in sight. My wife, two years my junior, was bringing in more money from her burgeoning matrimonial practice. Nothing like a bit of healthy domestic competition to motivate.

'Straightforward personal injuries case, Dermot. You should be able to manage it,' he patronises. 'Trip and fall. Nothing to it. Detailed consultation, 9.25.'

'And what about the Brief?' I ask plaintively. I like to make up the Brief the night before.

'Hardly any papers at all,' Arnold replies, 'I'll have them in the Library for you at 9.15.' (If the client only knew.)

Of course, when Arnold turns up in the morning, he is brandishing an untidy bundle of papers that could not be sorted in ten minutes, let alone read. If what masqueraded as a Brief had been placed in a bottle and shipped down to the Four Courts, it could not have arrived in a more untidy state.

Now one would not readily link Arnold with the musical life of the City. A post-prandial rugby chorus was about as close as he was ever likely to get to the Great Composers. He had sung a rousing version of 'The Drinking Song' on countless occasions in countless baths around the country without the slightest awareness of its provenance. George Frideric Handel would have been comfortably outside his repertoire, however. There may well have been times when he thought to himself, 'I did see all Heaven before me and the Great God Himself', but such times would have had neither a spiritual nor a musical inspiration.

On one occasion, their paths (Arnold and music, that is) had crossed, circumstantially at least, in the person of Rosie Barrett who worked in the markets. Rosie, one icy February morning, was making her way along Fishamble Street towards her place of work. It was early and since there was no-one around she was walking in the middle of the cobbled street, downhill towards the river. The Civic Offices had not yet raised their siamese heads above the level of the drawing board, so the Cathedral cast its shadow on her dark journey.

On the very spot where Handel's playing of the organ during the world première of 'Messiah' delighted the humble burgers and burgesses of Dublin, some centuries before, Rosie fell. Two cobbles, perhaps as long ago, had vacated their allotted place in the street tableau and Rosie was drawn inexorably to the vacancy. On her hands and knees, she made her way across the river and, with time, to No. 203 Gardiner Street. That was ten years closer in time to the first performance of 'Messiah'. Apparently, while according to Arnold a straightforward case, there had been some delay in the office in processing it.

At 75, Rosie was deafer and more stubborn than on the day of her accident. These conditions may not have been made worse by her fall, but she did sustain a nasty injury from which she never fully recovered; she had to use a walking stick and was nowhere near as confident or as mobile as she used to be. Lucky to be here at all, I suppose, so much time having elapsed since the accident.

★ ★ ★

I had an uneasy feeling about the case that I could not quite explain. Arnold insisted that it was 'straightforward'. Indeed, he had so informed the Client. Always a mistake. He had also informed her that her case was worth between £20,000 and £25,000. Another mistake. Her son, who was with her for moral support, had already spent the money. The fact that he was not with her on the day of the accident and, therefore, could be of no assistance in Court did not deter him from offering his advice.

Unfortunately, she had no witnesses. But that probably would not matter. She would be believed. Seventy-five-year-old women tend to be telling the truth or, more accurately, tend to be believed on the basis that, drawing closer in terms of time at any rate to the Ultimate Judge, they are less likely to be telling whoppers.

Notwithstanding the passage of time since the accident, Arnold never arranged for an engineer to examine the location and prepare a Report for the Court, complete with impressive map and photographs. This is the sort of detail that can swing a case. The Judge is flattered by the seriousness with which his Court is being taken and he also knows that the client is out-of-pocket so it fairly puts it up to him to dismiss the client's claim. Most judges would not regard Arnold's John Hinde postcard of Fishamble Street as an appropriate substitute for a fancy map and photographs. A very wise solicitor once told me, 'In Court, a hole is not dangerous until an engineer says it is.'

Despite the disadvantage then of the Plaintiff having no witnesses to the accident nor an engineer to deal with the self-explanatory hole, Rosie's case was, or so I was reminded by Arnold, 'straightforward': she fell into a hole in the road and she suffered injuries. What possible answer could there be?

Two answers, according to Michael Morrison, SC. A heavy in both the literal and metaphorical sense, he had been rolled out to defend this great cause. I had noticed him a little earlier and he had added to my unidentified foreboding about the case, but I had assumed that he was attached to a weightier matter. He had a confidential way of imparting information in between protracted pulls on the cigarette that was only out of his mouth for as long as he was physically in Court.

First of all, I was told, in that manner of his that suggests this information is for my ears only, that Dublin Corporation (the Defendant in this case and for whom he was acting) would be disputing liability. The Corpo had a reputation for fighting cases, so this in itself was not a surprise to me. The Corpo, he informed me most intimately, was not denying the existence of either Rosie or Fishamble Street or indeed the fact of the accident itself. It would be denying, however, that there was a hole in the street. According to the Corpo's Engineer, what Rosie called a hole was no more than the gap that you get between cobblestones. Millions of pedestrians had passed down that street since 'Messiah' was first performed without recorded mishap. Apparently Rosie was the first to fall.

He drew me even closer to him for the second answer, which I inferred was covered by the Official Secrets Act. He was playing at home now, having represented the Corporation on simply thousands of occasions and the pitch was familiar. The local rule called 'non-feasance'. The word rang a vague bell. Drawing with dedication on his cigarette, he explained without a hint of patronage that, somewhat anomalously, the Corporation was not liable if it had done no work at all. If the Corporation had repaired the street and repaired it badly, that would be misfeasance and the Plaintiff would recover – damages, if not her health. On the other hand, if the Corporation built the street properly in the first instance and thereafter left it to its own devices, then it would not be responsible if a hole appeared through wear and tear. That is, of course, if there was a hole at all and not just the designer gap that millions of pedestrians seemed to have avoided so skilfully over the centuries.

For these reasons, he confided in me, the Corporation would not be making any offer, but if we were prepared to withdraw our action, the Corporation would not pursue us for costs.

* * *

I thanked Mr. Morrison, SC, profusely for this information and returned crestfallen to my team. Arnold thought this was a lot of posturing on behalf of the Corporation, that I was overawed by Senior Counsel, and asked me did I not want to fight the case. His conviction was that the Judge's sympathy for a 75-year-old Plaintiff would overcome any anachronistic defence such as non-feasance.

How do you explain the nuances of non-feasance and misfeasance to a deaf and stubborn 75-year-old lady (whose every syllable could be heard in 'The Old Musick Hall' itself) outside the door of the Court minutes before the case is due to start? I try. At the top of her voice, she explains to me that her solicitor had told her she had a good case, otherwise she would not have come to Court, and anyway what had happened to the case since I came into it?

I returned to my colleague and reported my lack of progress. He very kindly hinted that he may be able to get me a small, all-in nuisance offer if I was interested. I tried to conceal my delight. After a short interval, he confirmed that to avoid all risks on his side he would be prepared to offer £5,000 all-in and that this figure was not negotiable.

Like some all-conquering hero, I returned to my team to announce the very satisfactory outcome to my negotiations. Unfortunately, I had not quite appreciated the depth of the chasm which had developed between me on the one hand and Arnold, the Client and her son on the other. The Client thought the offer was insulting and told me she was not interested in a penny less than £25,000 and that she was here to get Justice and Justice she would get.

I argued with her, raising my copious eyebrows in a most sincere way to try to convey to her the gravity of the situation and the fact that she was throwing good money away. I restrained myself from mentioning that she was throwing my money away also – as this was my only hope of getting paid (not, of course, that this influenced my advice) – on the basis that such a remark would be less than professional. I told her that there was little doubt but that she would lose this case and end up with nothing and that Mr. Morrison, SC, agreed with me. To no avail. 'Insulting . . . not a penny less than . . . Justice . . .'

I didn't need to convey this reply to my learned friend because he heard every word of it, as did, I am sure, His Lordship, quietly doing the crossword in his chambers on the other side of an open window. However, out of courtesy, I crossed the corridor and conveyed. More Official Secrets and into Court.

* * *

A mere formality. There was just one case between us and Judge O'Mahoney who would have been a good draw from Rosie's point of view. Judge O'Mahoney was pro-Plaintiff by nature, having had a Plaintiff-based practice all his working life, and vehemently anti-local authority by experience, having suffered ignominiously at their hands on more than one occasion when acting for Plaintiffs whose cases were founded more on hope than on law.

Unfortunately, that one case remained between us and the good Judge O'Mahoney. Instead, we were sent to Judge Crotty, who was as good a draw for the Corpo as O'Mahoney had been for us. Crotty was at the end of a long and not very distinguished career on the Bench and was tired. He was knocking off the days on his calendar until retirement. For a long time now, he had been quite unsympathetic to Plaintiffs and, in addition, was difficult to appear before. Anyway, for the next hour or two, Judge Crotty would be the focus of our attention.

Crotty's disposition was revealed in all its glory almost immediately: 'Mrs. Barrett, this accident happened in 1981. It is now 1991. Ten years later.' (Brilliant Judge. But wasted in the Circuit Court. Tip-off the AG. An 'A' in maths obviously.) 'Why has it taken so long to get your action on for trial?' continued His Lordship.

'What?' says Mrs. Barrett, loudly. 'I'm sorry, Judge, I can't hear a word you're saying.'

I offered to diffuse the situation. 'My client is hard of hearing,

My Lord. Perhaps I can explain for her?'

'There'd better be an explanation, Mr. McNamara. Ten years is a long time,' Judge Crotty added, revealing consistency of intellectual alertness.

'Of course, My Lord. The explanation is quite simply that the solicitor handling Mrs. Barrett's case left the office.'

'But that was five years ago,' interposed the hard-of-hearing Mrs. Barrett.

'Be quiet, madam! When was that, Mr. McNamara? When did he leave?'

'About 1986, My Lord.'

'That doesn't explain a ten-year delay.'

'Unfortunately, the file went missing, My Lord. Murphy's Law!'

'It's not very satisfactory, Mr. McNamara. One interpretation of the delay could be that your solicitor had very little confidence in Mrs. Barrett's case. I am not saying that is the position, Mr. McNamara, but it's certainly open to that interpretation,' commented Crotty, continuing his flair for perspicacity.

'Oh no, Judge!' interjected Mrs. Barrett, whose hearing loss was apparently in remission. 'Mr. O'Reilly assured me that I had a very good case.'

I so wanted to corroborate Mrs. Barrett by informing His Lordship of the negotiations that had taken place and how Arnold had obstructed the settlement that was on offer.

'Anyway, I'll accept your explanation, Mr. McNamara. *De bene esse.* I'll put these observations out of my mind and I will refrain from jumping to conclusions.' How magnanimous he was. How wise and learned. What intellectual restraint.

'May it please your Lordship.'

Mrs. Barrett continued with her evidence, but not for long.

'Mr. McNamara, is there an engineer in this case? Is there a map? Do you have photographs? Am I to try this case in blinkers?'

'A hole is after all a hole, My Lord,' I thought to myself. But I said, 'In normal circumstances, the accident locus would have been inspected by an engineer and Your Lordship would have the benefit of a map and photographs.' My instinct for survival momentarily overtaken by an irresistible desire to attribute the responsibility for the errors in this case, I added, 'In this case, my solicitor felt that as

Fishamble Street was so well-known, an engineer's examination would be superfluous.'

'Superfluous, Mr. McNamara?'

'Perhaps I can be of assistance,' intervened Mr. Morrison, SC, obsequiously. 'I have a map and photographs which I will be proving when I go into evidence, if we get that far. Perhaps I can make them available at this stage?'

'Thank you, Mr. Morrison. It's no more than I would have expected from your client.'

Mrs. Barrett proceeded with her evidence, in the course of which she managed to convince Crotty that her deafness was more convenient than real. We were not doing very well, even on the merits. We barely cleared Mr. Morrison's application for a direction. He then called a witness to say how many people would travel this street every year. Followed by his engineer. He was probably home even before opening a line of authorities, many of which predated the street itself, which spelt out the doctrine that would give the Plaintiff the Justice she sought so dearly and so dearly deserved. Mr. Morrison, SC, had even brought along a copy of each report for the Judge himself, peppering his submissions with comments like 'As Your Lordship well knows' and 'Your Lordship will be familiar with', as if we needed reminding that in his own days at the Bar His Lordship's main client had been the Corporation and his main ally the defence of non-feasance.

* * *

A foregone conclusion. His Lordship held that the case was unstateable, both on the law and on the merits. He dismissed the claim with costs.

My client went on the attack before I had a chance to convey to her my humble opinion that she was a foolish old woman who had been offered a present of £5,000 and had turned it down. Before I had a chance to deliver myself of these less than objective, but no less accurate, observations, she wanted to know why *I* had lost the 'straightforward' case her solicitor told her she had. She supposed it was my fault the case took so long to get to Court and that there was no engineer, and anyway why didn't I have all the books the other side had? So much for the deafness.

With admirable restraint I bit my upper lip, thanked the ungrateful pedestrian for her comments and excused myself. As I walked down the corridor, I wondered if Arnold had a 'D' team.

There were few evenings that I didn't get a phone call at 6.25. This was one of them.

★ ★ ★

4

Will we need Moriarty as a witness?

Mostly, Arnold only became aware of his case for the following day on the evening before. Mostly therefore, my involvement with the case only began with a phone call at 6.25 in the evening. Occasionally, Arnold's natural flair for inefficiency broke down and the Brief fell in my letterbox two weeks in advance. This premature briefing had its disadvantages. Firstly, there was a risk of mislaying (barristers never lose) the Brief. Secondly, Arnold would ring me twice a day for the fortnight, religiously morning and evening, with queries about the case.

Solicitors fall into two categories. There are those who phone you only in the Law Library and those who phone you only at home. Arnold fell into the latter category. It was as if he did not realise the Library had a phone service. No doubt there are antiquated features to the Law Library, but the absence of a phone service is not one of them. In fact, Arnold was in his office between seven and nine in the morning and between five and seven in the evening. I suspect that if he wasn't in Court he took the rest of the day off. The explanation for the out-of-hours phone calls was therefore that it suited his schedule.

It never occurred to Arnold that he might be disturbing you. Working on another Brief, feeding a baby or simply viewing 'Baywatch'. Maybe even telling your wife over an aperitif that you were about to leave her and run away with her best friend in the Library (or, of course, in these politically correct days, vice versa).

From the moment the Brief was despatched from his office, Arnold acquired a proprietorial interest in you. He adopted you, for a short time. He was on Page 106 of the Brief and you must be too. Some problem, real or imagined, had arisen. Arnold was grappling with it and he assumed you were too. It never occurred to him that you would be other than on top of the Brief on a 24-hour basis from the moment it arrived. He was not aware of the reality, which was that the Brief was never read until the night before. He never apologised for the interruption. Quite the reverse. Puzzlement, if there was the slightest hint of hesitation from you in handling the query. The apology was much more likely to come from you.

The query most times would be trivial but occasionally would require some consideration. Like all solicitors, Arnold assumed that the answers would flow as naturally and spontaneously to you as the questions to him. I seem to recall Mrs. Gandhi saying, not to me personally, that whereas there was a time in the long ago when she had all the answers, now that she was older, she had only questions. (Now that she is no longer with us, perhaps she has all the answers once again.) Arnold and Mrs. Gandhi would have got on well together. Arnold, too, had only questions. But whether that had anything to do with getting older or wiser I had my doubts. Even Mrs. Gandhi might have had her Eastern patience tested by Arnold's morning and evening routine.

Impatience with your solicitor is not a recognised career move. You will be tempted, of course. Many times a day you will be tempted. Unlike Oscar, the temptation must be resisted. Your experience as a barrister over the years equips you to resist. From time to time, however, one cracks. In fact, the Bench is littered with former colleagues who failed to resist – they cracked, in time lost their painstakingly acquired practice and were forced to apply for the Bench.

There is a natural tension between solicitors and barristers, and it is this: all solicitors regard their barristers as stupid. The explanation for the barrister's selection is simply that the solicitor perceives him to be not quite as stupid as the rest. When the barrister asks a question of witness or client in consultation, the solicitor intercepts it contemptuously, making it clear that if the barrister had read his Brief properly the question would have been quite unnecessary.

The solicitor really comes into his own in Court. When cross-examination is not going his barrister's way, the clever solicitor quickly comes to his rescue with volumes of explanatory memoranda. These soon exceed the Brief and so confuse the wandering barrister that he loses his way entirely and resumes his seat. If, by any fluke, the barrister wins the case, the result was never in doubt. If he loses, it is made clear where the fault lies and an ominous silence descends on the relationship until the next time the solicitor's A, B and C teams let him down at the last moment.

* * *

This particular Brief arrived two weeks in advance. There was a covering letter, all of two lines long, and the original file. Upside down and back to front. Not a typed document in sight. Original vouchers dropping out. No mention of exclusive attention, but this was certainly implied from previous dealings. And tested that very evening, at 9.05, just in the middle of the UEFA Cup Final.

The exchange went as usual. 'Is that you, Dermot?' (Who else?) 'Will we need Moriarty as a witness?'

I hadn't the faintest idea what Arnold was talking about or who Moriarty was, still less whether or not we needed him as a witness. I couldn't have known without reading the entire Brief which, with two weeks to go, would have been a complete waste of time. I asked a few searching questions and then chanced my arm by telling Arnold, 'It might be just as well to have him'.

There is, of course, a procedure for acquiring this information and it is to ask Counsel to advise proofs for the hearing. A sort of checklist, witnesses, documents, that sort of thing. Not very expensive, but Arnold is into making small savings.

As, for example, the 'consultation room'. Arnold doesn't bother with a room for his 'detailed consultation, 9.35'. This saving has a number of hidden advantages. For one, the consultation now has to take place in the crowded lobby outside the Law Library, affectionately known as 'The Square Hall', which is about as comfortable and private as Heuston Station. This is a good idea because there is a reasonable chance that, unbeknown to you, your opposition is consulting right beside you. In this way, you can share the frailties of your case with the other side before going into Court so that whatever advantage accompanies the element of surprise will be eliminated.

Secondly, have you ever taken notes with your notebook placed on your raised thigh as you balance on one leg like a bewigged flamingo?

For once the 'detailed' consultation so close to Arnold's heart takes place on time. Arnold is there and, with him, as ever, a host of golden witnesses. Most of these will be hopelessly irrelevant, but it will be another half hour before the full extent of their irrelevance is revealed. The simplest process of elimination would be to ask each witness why he is here and if a vacant expression comes over his face to return him to the workforce. I can't do this, however, because if it is that obvious that he is unnecessary it would be embarrassing for Arnold to have him expelled so unceremoniously. More embarrassing for me if he has travelled from Malin Head or Rio de Janeiro on the strength of my telling Arnold on the phone the other night that 'It might be just as well to have him'.

The case is all about a stabbing incident in a pub near Belleville, appropriately called 'The End of the Road'. Judging by the number at the consultation, the pub must run a World Cup match every night of the week. We had the owner of the pub, the former owner, the owner's wife (none of whom were there on the night in question and none of whom could offer one scintilla of relevant evidence in the case), barmen who were on-duty, barmen who were off-duty, witnesses who were there that night, the previous night, the following night. In all, twenty witnesses. I said to Arnold that in future he might arrange his consultations for 7.35. He was not sure if I was serious or joking, and so conjured up an expression that purported to cover both possibilities.

But where was Moriarty? Arnold had not told me that Moriarty's long-arranged family holiday in Florida was being interrupted at the Client's expense to allow him to attend. Had I known that the other night, I would have devoted more consideration to his attendance than 'It might be just as well to have him'.

One thing that cannot be said about Arnold, whether in consultation or in Court, is that he remains idle. Quite the contrary. He writes furiously, head to paper. He is even writing when nothing is being said. In the unlikely event of Claudia Schiffer bursting into the consultation, Arnold would not be distracted from his task. True professionalism. I often wonder what he is writing because occasionally when it has been necessary to consult Counsel's or Solicitor's note of the evidence, Arnold's note has been so wide of the mark as to suggest that his presence in Court is merely physical.

As distilled at the consultation, the facts of this case appeared to me to be as follows: Mr. O'Driscoll owns 'The End of the Road' pub in Belleville. Every Sunday night a cabaret is held upstairs, a family affair for all the generations. The pub is a well-run establishment which prides itself on its anonymity, in the sense of being unknown to the Gardai. Until this Sunday evening, that is. At approximately 11pm a fight broke out, quite without warning according to my witnesses. A neutral patron was stabbed with a six-inch blade. The staff responded swiftly and heroically, and order was restored in a matter of minutes. By the time the Gardai arrived, the entertainment had resumed and you would not have known that anything out of the ordinary had occurred.

Mr. Declan Duffy, better known as 'Deco', was the injured patron and he was now suing Mr. O'Driscoll, trading as 'The End of the Road', for damages for his injuries due to the inadequate supervision of premises and patrons.

I spent an appropriate amount of time questioning each potential witness until I had sifted the relevant from the irrelevant. By consultation's end, Moriarty still had not arrived. The word was that his plane had been delayed at Shannon and if he arrived at all it would be after the case had started. Moriarty was the manager on-duty on the night and, according to his short hand-written statement, he would say that there was nothing unusual about the evening, the patrons were enjoying and behaving themselves as they usually did. I didn't like the idea of calling witnesses without having had a consultation with them, but it looked as if Moriarty would be safe enough.

* * *

We were listed in Court 6 before Judge Horan. This was good news for my Client. Judge Horan was not noted for his pro-Plaintiff tendencies. In fact, his two prejudices were Plaintiffs and drink, in either order. He was anti-both. It was not clear whether he would more oppose the consumer of alcohol (the Plaintiff) or the dispenser (the Defendant).

When he was elevated to the Bench, his friends at the Bar asked a well-known cartoonist to do a portrait of him as a presentation. But the cartoonist refused on the basis that there were no distinguishing physical features; he was too ordinary in appearance for caricature. If Judge Horan was undistinguished physically, it did not follow that he was without a Bench persona. That would indeed be to underestimate the man.

When he sat each day at 10.30 he would call over the List, which in itself would take an inordinate length of time. Counsel in each case would estimate the length of time that each case was likely to take. The Judge would then total the estimated number of hours, point out that there were only four Court hours into which to fit eight hours of cases, announce that even he could not solve this particular problem and, with a gesture which suggested the fatuity of the legal system, leave the Bench. A coffee and a crossword later, the Senior Barrister present would venture into his chambers and inform the judicial luminary that it had been very helpful of him to afford time to the various parties before him and that that time has been used most gainfully, a number of cases had settled, the List was now reduced to more manageable proportions, and if His Lordship saw fit it would be helpful if he would sit to rule the settlements and perhaps take up the remainder of the List. As the clock was now closing on 1pm, Judge Horan saw little harm in this course and sat.

Thus was 'List Management' interpreted by Judge Horan. Not unsuccessfully, one might add, because, unlikely as it may seem, his List was cleared every evening before 4pm.

He lived on the south side of the Liffey and only crossed it out of dire necessity. It would have suited him better if the Law Library had stayed in Dublin Castle. In recent times, a Circuit Court had begun to sit in Temple Bar, on the site of the old Dolphin Hotel. He eyed the venue wistfully and would probably have gone there were it not for the superiority of his chambers in the Four Courts. In his experience, most Plaintiffs were either working or drinking class, or both, and these were distinct handicaps coming into his Court.

* * *

If I said that he sat at 10.30, then I misled you. The punctuality that he insisted on for everyone else did not apply to him. He would sit at any moment between 10.30 and 10.45. This is very troublesome for Counsel because at that precise hour they are juggling a number of matters and depend on the Courts sitting promptly to avoid being caught in two or more Courts at the same time. Judges have such short memories.

On this occasion, Judge Horan's lateness was appreciated. Arnold had an irritating habit of disappearing at the very moment when he was most needed. I never knew where he had gone or why. Occasionally I would be walking down the corridor with him towards the Court where our case was listed. We would be discussing the case. Suddenly I would realise I had been talking to myself and that Arnold had vanished. I would look around and behold a corridor utterly without trace of Arnold. I would retrace my steps, enter another Court and discover Arnold there, as disorientated as a lost tourist. This would explain some disappearances. But not this one. I had no idea where he went on this occasion or whether or when he would return. Anyway he did, just in time to hear the Registrar announce '*Duffy v. O'Driscoll*, trading as "End of the Road".'

'Going on, My Lord, two hours.'

The case was not going smoothly from the Plaintiff's point of view. Deco was a rough-looking diamond, partially obscured by tattoos and sporting an ear-ring. Not exactly His Lordship's cup of tea. No earthly reason why he couldn't tell the truth as well as the next man, but certainly not what His Lordship had in mind by way of a son-in-law. Of course, Deco wasn't himself to blame in any way – for the fight, that is. Presumably he had some responsibility for his appearance. He was an innocent victim, but he needed to win the Judge's sympathy if the considerable problems on liability were to be overcome. His Lordship enquired if the other scars on his face were also acquired in this incident. Apparently not. As His Lordship thought. Nor did the Judge think much of Deco's insistence that he had only drunk two pints in the entire evening. Of all the gods in heaven, Bacchus was not the Judge's favourite.

Deco's Counsel was not advancing his cause. He was represented by George O'Malley, BL. Now George's self-confidence (high), a euphemism for arrogance, was in inverse proportion to his ability (low). Add to that fatal cocktail just a soupçon of short-temperedness and you have the picture.

The principal maxim of the oral tradition of the Bar is 'Never blame your solicitor'. Blame everyone else in sight, but never your solicitor. Some hoo-ha had just broken out (just as suddenly as the fight in 'The End of the Road') between George and the Judge in relation to pleadings. The heat was off me momentarily and I relaxed in my friend's discomfiture. But not for long.

'The problem is not on my side of the Bench,' I heard George pronounce with a fine sense of demarcation.

His solicitor looked in my direction. The Judge looked in my direction. With an inferiority complex nurtured over thirty years of being in the wrong, I looked in my direction. What had I done now? The only person in Court not looking in my direction was George. Staring poker-faced straight in front of him. Could he be blaming the Judge? Even worse. He was glowering at the by-now cowering figure of his solicitor, at last exposed as the problem 'not on my [George's] side of the Bench'.

The cardinal rule was not just being broken. It was being ruthlessly smashed and in the public glare of open Court. The moment represented the full and final flowering of George's hitherto well-concealed, but long-suspected stupidity. I wasn't to know that within a month we would have a new Judge.

Still no sign of Moriarty. George closed his case. In an ideal world, I would have called Moriarty first as the manager on-duty to set the scene with some authority and seniority. In his absence, I called the head barman on-duty. The defence stumbled momentarily when he identified his occupation as 'bar person'. Feminism had by-passed His Lordship who was happy with the English language as it stood. The barman recovered well. He was adamant that there had been no hint of trouble and, if a drink was served, he hardly noticed. The teddy bears' picnic was a more robust affair. Not surprisingly, George felt that the witness was overstating the peace and quiet, and put it to him that things were not quite so civilised leading up to the fateful hour.

This line of cross-examination was interrupted by the good Judge who, summoning every drop of snobbery in his blue-blooded veins, pointed out to George, 'Mr. O'Malley, this is a pub in Belleville we are talking about, not Claridges'. George, incandescent with rage, muttering not quite sotto voce about His Lordship's unfitness to be on the Bench, resumed his seat. The straws in the wind were blowing in the direction of 'The End of the Road'.

* * *

As I wondered about my next witness, Arnold passed me a note saying that Moriarty had just walked in the door. I had a decision to make and not a lot of time to make it. 'Never ask a question you do not know the answer to' runs the golden rule of advocacy. A fortiori, 'Do not call a witness if you do not know what he is going to say'. This was a strong argument against calling him. Furthermore, the case was running well and would we not win it without him?

The evidence established that the evening had been uneventful until the incident, which therefore could not have been anticipated, and the staff had reacted without delay to the outbreak of violence. What more could the publican have done? On the other hand, the Judge might be a bit suspicious if we didn't call the man in charge on the night and anyway hadn't he come all the way back from Florida for the case because I had said 'It might be just as well to have him'.

'Come up, Mr. Moriarty.'

He presented well, shirt and tie, that sort of thing, unadorned by tattoo or ear-ring, gave his evidence in a matter-of-fact sort of way. He backed up the evidence of the head barman in all material respects, differing slightly here and there, thereby conferring greater authenticity on what he had to say. The defence looked watertight. George was merely going through the motions.

George was coming to the end of his scoreless cross-examination. 'Were either of these gladiators known to you before the night?' a resigned George enquired.

'The man who done the stabbing, I knew him,' came the unexpected reply.

His Lordship, who was well into a mental draft of his Judgment at this stage, almost missed the reply. But not quite.

'And how did you know him?' the aroused Judge asked.

'He had been banned from the pub for six months for starting a fight,' said Moriarty.

Fresh with his Florida tan, Moriarty was oblivious to the implications of what he had said. Not so George who, with the last kick of the game, had got himself into extra time and was now going for gold.

'And why did you let him in?' George cut loose.

'It was coming to the end of the six months and he had some story about a wedding anniversary.' All the way from Florida for these little gems.

The mental draft of the Judgment was hastily rewritten and Deco the Plaintiff, tattooed and ear-ringed, got home. By the time we reached the corridor, Moriarty was on the plane back to Florida. Arnold had a parting question – 'Did we have to call Moriarty?'

★ ★ ★

5

An Eye on the Whiplash

The sources of my modest practice never cease to amaze me. Never the fellow you sat beside at school who, with wasted foresight, you allowed plagiarise your examination paper in the Leaving Cert. Never the pal with whom you spent most of your college hours in Hartigan's, swopping women or stories of women. Never the family friend who every Christmas morning over drinks in your home enquires what you are doing now and when you tell him for the third Christmas morning in a row that you are studying for the Bar, without as much as a pause as a concession of sorts to truth, replies that he will send you his entire practice. Even less likely, if that is possible, any member of your family.

May God smile gently on the soul of my beloved late uncle who, on being introduced to me in the course of my third year at the Bar, professed ignorance of the fact that his nephew was in the Library and, in the same untruthful breath, assured me that he would keep an eye on me and when I had established myself he would be the first to brief me. So much for the old boys' network.

Mr. Wilkinson was indeed an honourable exception. At least he had given me a chance, even if I had blown it as high as the Four Courts itself in the course of my first Brief, *DPP v. Wilkinson*. Furthermore, he had introduced me to my first solicitor, J. Arnold O'Reilly. Even if Arnold and I did not rate one another very highly, we were useful to one another, for the moment in any event. From Arnold's point of view, not many of his team could offer 24-hour availability. He could, with some confidence, expect to find me at any hour of the day occupying a seat just inside the main entrance to the Library, for all the world like some Dutch whore confirming the availability of her wares to the passing world. If not there, then certainly sipping a lingering coffee in the Barristers' Restaurant, once again in full view of kerb-crawling solicitors, unlike the more successful of my colleagues who would make sure to be out of sight.

From my point of view, Arnold, from time to time, took the blank look off my diary. I was sure that as time passed and inevitable success beckoned, fancier solicitors from fancier offices would come my way. In the meantime, be not proud. Arnold's Brief was better than no brief.

One of my contemporaries worked for one such fancy office. From an early stage he was catapulted into a fashionable practice. Within weeks of his arrival in the Library, he was on every conceivable insurance panel. He was never accused of doing anything to discourage the work. Quite the contrary. If the odd meal here or there with the even odder insurance man or woman would do anything, no matter how small, to enhance his practice, then there was no-one at the Bar who was better known to the restauranteurs of Dublin. There were those of his colleagues who said that his early success at the Bar was in inverse proportion to his ability. But then they would, wouldn't they?

The solicitors in such fancy offices had long since adopted even fancier parlance. For example, they attended 'conferences', not 'consultations'. In time, their barristers discovered that they could mark higher fees by attending conferences rather than the more mundane consultations attended by the rest of us mere mortals. Another example, you never got through to these eminences on an ordinary phone. It was always the 'conference phone'. You had the impression that the solicitor was in the middle of a very important meeting and was really only talking to you as a great favour or, alternatively, that he was surrounded by numerous important people, each of whom was analysing every word of your advice – in either event, not very relaxing. That is, of course, if you got by the telephonist in the first instance who wanted to know every intimacy of your business before even putting you through to the solicitor's secretary.

Anyway, it was really the Brief from the fancy office that I wanted to speak of. It arrives in the form of a hardback folder. Inside, an index, each page paginated. Each section of the Brief flagged with a different colour. A divider separating each document. Every document, no matter how irrelevant, will be included. The documentation will be in chronological order. The first document will be a Case to Counsel, which will purport to be a summary of the case but more likely will be a repetition thereof. In short, no expense spared – for the Brief from the fancy office is a work of art.

The Brief from Arnold's office, on the other hand, is less pretentious. It sort of falls out of the end of the large brown envelope which itself is coming to the end of its recycled existence, the recycling owing less to the concept of environmental friendship than to frugality. There is no covering letter, no index, no pagination. The first thing to do is to separate personal and other correspondence that has been included in error. Then it is essential to impose some chronology on the unwieldy file, which is difficult when half of the documents are undated. Original vouchers should be isolated. Endeavour to read hand-written attendances, which make prescriptions look like calligraphy. Naturally, many crucial documents have been sent to someone else and if you phone Arnold to ask about them, you will be told you are fussing.

The final humiliation is the line through the names of several other barristers who, for one understandable reason or another, were unable to accept the Brief.

* * *

Sometime, somewhat longer than immediately, the facts of the case begin to emerge. Suzanne Bell, the Plaintiff, is a 35-year-old married woman living in a cul-de-sac in Rathmines. At the time of her accident, she was working as manageress in an upmarket night-club in Temple Bar called 'Rollers'. She was opening a bottle of Chateau Neuf du Pape for a member when she suffered a hyper-extension injury to her neck – an injury expensively known to Irish jurisprudence as the 'whiplash' and thank God for it, because it has reared many a barrister's family. Her whiplash was caused, she alleged, by a combination of a defective bottle-opener and a cork that had been fitted too tightly, rather like those figures you see poured into jeans many sizes too small for the wearer. She was suing her employer, the owner of 'Rollers', who was insured by Mr. Wilkinson's company. That's where Arnold and I came in.

There were a few features of the case which did not recommend themselves to Mr. Wilkinson. No-one else in the night-club witnessed the accident. Ms. Bell continued working as usual, without complaint, until the club closed around the time of early Mass. It was a week before she made any report of the accident and during that week she worked without apparent compromise.

In addition, there was a serious conflict of medical evidence. According to her pleadings, the Plaintiff was suffering constant 'exquisite' pain in her neck. She couldn't turn her head. She had to wear a cervical collar at all times. It was now five years since the accident and she was not getting any better. If anything, she was getting worse. She had been for physiotherapy. She had even tried acupuncture, which would not be to her advantage in some courts which regarded such brands of alternative medicine as closely akin to witchcraft. She had received nerve blocks and had attended a pain-management course. There was nothing she had not tried in her pursuit of health, yet only short-term relief was achieved and the prognosis was 'guarded'. Her sex life was reduced by 80% and, on the work front, she was not going to be able to resume her pre-accident employment. This Plaintiff was reaching for the stars.

In contrast, our orthopaedic surgeon took the view that she was long since recovered from a non-bony, soft-tissue injury and if there were any continuing symptoms she was grossly exaggerating them. Every conceivable test known to the Blackrock Clinic had been carried out without identifying any physical cause of her symptoms, which were purely subjective. In short, she was a fraud.

If there was any doubt about this, the report of the private investigator settled it. Arnold was in a state of high excitement when he called me to the Library door at 9.25 on the morning of the case. He had a tendency to over-identify with his client. He accepted as gospel what he was told by his witnesses and never entertained even the possibility of their fallibility, innocent or otherwise. This over-identification was expected of his Counsel too, which made the task of giving the client independent advice rather hazardous. Advice which tended to undermine the client's aspirations in regard to his or her case was looked on as nothing short of treachery. 'Whose side are you on anyway?' and 'Where's your bottle?' were not untypical Arnold responses to pointing out the weaknesses on our side of the fence.

'Had I read the medical reports? Had I seen the PI's report?' Arnold asked rhetorically. He hadn't the slightest interest in my view of the case. Indeed, there couldn't be any view other than his. 'A try-on if ever I saw one,' he intoned. 'Mr. Wilkinson will be pleased.' It would have been a brave barrister of six-years' standing who would have disagreed with Arnold at this moment and bravery was not my most obvious virtue.

In any event, I was beginning to reach for the stars myself at this stage. I could smell a major success. Promotion within Mr. Wilkinson's panel? Inclusion on his panel in one of his fancy offices? Who knows where it might all end?

★ ★ ★

Arnold called Henry Fitzmartin, SC. Now no-one would have dreamt of calling Henry Harry. He was not that kind of Henry. A Silk of some significance, according to himself. If I were to say that he was a serious-minded barrister, that would be to lend to the meaning of the word 'serious' a certain levity that Henry did not possess. If the word 'gravitas' had not been invented, then it surely would have been once Henry arrived. It oozed out of his every pore. It was not a natural gravitas, however. It was most cultivated.

Henry never 'thought' anything. He was 'of the opinion that' or 'would be inclined to think that' or 'had formed a view that'. He liked to listen to things *de bene esse*. References to the Treaty of Rome and his appearances before the European Court peppered his elegant conversation. He liked being a barrister, performed everything as he believed a true barrister ought and whether in a bus (unlikely) or at a theatre everyone around him would have known immediately that he was a member of the Irish Bar. He laughed little and certainly not at anything you or I might think funny. It wasn't that he was vertically challenged, but to have been a little taller would have suited his self-image and he would not have had to stretch quite as much.

Henry did not regard personal injury cases as real work. They were filed in that section of his practice which he liked to refer to as 'recreational'. I was in awe of such self-confidence. I was in awe of Henry. I had not been led by him before. In fact, I had not been led by very many before because, if the truth were to be told, my High Court practice was a little slow in getting off the ground.

As I waited with Arnold and Mr. Wilkinson for the arrival of Henry, my immediate concern was whether or not Henry would know me. I had my wig and gown on, so the chances were that he would realise I was his Junior. But would he know my name? I was concerned, in front of Mr. Wilkinson, that I might not be known by my Senior. It would not say very much for how I was doing. It wasn't long before it was clear that I was right to be concerned.

'Good morning, Arnold. Good morning, Mr. Wilkinson. Welcome to the Bar, David, who are you devilling with?' greeted Henry Fitzmartin, SC.

'Well, actually, I have finished devilling, Henry – five years ago,' I replied, my worst fears confirmed.

'Goodness me, how out of touch one gets moving between Luxembourg and Dublin! What room are we in, Arnold?'

As we settled into the inadequate consultation room, somewhere below the bowels of the Four Courts, I noticed Henry's hardback folder, Arnold's concession to Henry's posh practice. I wondered if it were the only concession. The Assistant Manager of 'Rollers' night-club was doing his best to set the scene. I did not expect that Henry would have graced 'Rollers' with his presence, but I did think that he would have heard of Temple Bar. He seemed to be under the misapprehension that Temple Bar had something to do with the Inns of Court in London, where he to-ed and fro-ed. 'Le Cirque', another well-known night-club in Dublin, would probably have suggested to him a French subtitle at the Film Theatre. To his cerebral taste, a night on the town was more likely to conjure up a session in the Concert Hall, followed by hot chocolate in The Conrad. Certainly, a hop in Bective or Lansdowne in the fifties was as close as he had ever got to 'Rollers'. For this reason, it took a little time to convey to him the precise ambience of the locus in quo.

We had a strong team. Every employee of 'Rollers' was present. No-one had witnessed Suzanne's accident. No-one even knew about it until a week later. To a man and a woman, the staff was prepared to stand up and tell the truth, the whole truth and nothing but the truth. Our engineer was one of the better ones: he had found nothing wrong with the bottle-opener, indeed thousands of bottles had been opened and never such an accident. Even if the accident happened at all, and this must be in doubt, surely as a matter of law, the engineer pontificated, it was unforeseeable that opening a bottle of Chateau Neuf du Pape could give rise to a life-long whiplash. I was sure that Henry would be grateful for the engineer's exposition of the legal principle of foreseeability. The doctor was on stand-by, but we had his very clear report as to the Plaintiff's recovery. And, of course, there was the jewel in the defence crown, namely, the private investigator (who couldn't attend the consultation because he had some observations to make in relation to other cases on his way in).

At about 10.20, Henry opined. And very much along the lines of what Mr. Wilkinson and Arnold wanted to hear. He saw no reason to resile from his formal opinion. The case would have to be fought.

Henry was gathering up his papers. I hardly heard him say 'And what do you think?' (without the courtesy of even my wrong name) and, if I did, I never for one moment thought that the question was addressed to me. I was sitting beside Mr. Wilkinson and assumed that Henry was diplomatically seeking his view. The enquiry was followed by silence, a prolonged silence, that eventually began to puzzle me until at last the guinea dropped and I realised that all eyes were on me.

'Who? Me?' I heard myself say as if from a disembodied distance, to be greeted by hoots of laughter. Even the humourless Henry permitted himself the hint of a smile. Mr. Wilkinson seemed to find the exchange particularly amusing.

We headed for the Round Hall, that cathedral of marketplaces off which are carved four principal altars of Justice and on top of which, like a great wig, the tailored dome rests.

★ ★ ★

The course of justice is not predictable. The watertight case of the night before in the light of day begins to leak. The cold Brief says nothing of the Plaintiff's three previous accidents or, worse, convictions. No mention of the fact that he or she was collecting dole and social welfare at the same time. For some reason best known to your client, he or she thinks that it would be better if you received these little gems of information at one minute to eleven from your opposite number, just as the curtain goes up and down simultaneously. One of the great sources of information about your case is, very often, your opposite number.

There are many factors in the legal equation. Some are contained in your instructions. Some more become apparent at consultation and more when you talk to the other side. Some can be anticipated. Some cannot. The good barrister is alive to the permutations of litigation. The not-so-good barrister is not.

From time to time, there will emerge in a case a feature in the face of which the opposition will be helpless. Ms. Suzanne Bell was one such feature. She came into focus for the first time the moment we entered the great marketplace. It was 10.55. The call-over of the day's List had just taken place. This was the high point of the day. The Round Hall resembled a cocktail party. Packed with barristers, solicitors, clients, witnesses, insurance people, doctors, engineers, hardly a sphere of professional life was not represented. Last-minute instructions were bespoken, the business of barter begun. And yet somehow, in the midst of this crowded tapestry of courtly life, in a manner known only to superstars, Ms. Bell managed to create her own time and space.

What was it about her that commanded such attention? Was it her pouty lips? Her ample figure? Her long summer legs? Her pleated mini-skirt that reached only as far as St. Patrick's Day? So short that, were it white, she could have stepped straight onto the Centre Court at Wimbledon. Even her cervical collar looked like it were an extension of her lingerie. This goddess, whose gesticulation of hand and leg added greatly to her conversation – and everyone else's. Consultations were cut short in mid-sentence as she was spotted for the first time. Negotiations were interrupted. Clients may have thought that their cases were getting an airing between their Counsel and perhaps they were, but not at this moment. Ms. Bell did not merely illustrate that something in litigation that made it unpredictable, that unknown factor upon which cases turn, that hidden dynamic – she defined it.

'I will send *Bell v. Rollers* to Mr. Justice Fleming,' the President of the High Court had said, as he assigned the day's List. Ms. Bell did not need luck. Whether she liked it or not, luck was thrust upon her in the guise of His Lordship.

Fleming J – one of those few people in life who is excessively gifted. Tennis international. John Brooke scholar. And now Judge of the High Court. Everything came easily to him and nothing more easily than women. The trouble was that he was too talented to be a Judge. The Bench did not extend him. He had too much time on his hands. And too many hands. Two too many. And he would be better off keeping them to himself. If he hadn't been to 'Rollers', it was only a matter of time. No danger of catching Fleming J in the Concert Hall. Come to think of it, if the Judge and Henry exchanged playgrounds for an evening, it would have done neither of them any harm. In drawing Mr. Justice Fleming, Ms. Bell had done her case no harm at all. Her Counsel knew that, but did Henry?

Negotiations commenced, but were short-lived. 'The Plaintiff is looking for £150,000,' Henry told us. Now Henry had previously furnished an opinion where he 'was inclined to think' that, in the unlikely event of the Plaintiff succeeding, her award would be in the region of £30,000, bearing in mind the reports of our doctor and private eye. Not much room there for negotiation, particularly when Henry was not one to take his own opinion lightly.

Was I the only member of our team with a reservation, I wondered? However, mustering all the courage I could command, I managed to keep this to myself. It was unlikely that Mr. Wilkinson would hear from Arnold any view other than that which he, Mr. Wilkinson, wished to hear and, as for Henry, he seemed to be as oblivious to everything extraneous to his formal opinion as he was to the enchantment of Ms. Bell. And so, into the valley of death.

We turned towards Court. As we did so, I asked Arnold if there was any sign of the PI. He pointed towards one of the pillars. I could just make out the left-hand side of a Clouseau-like figure. Only the parrot was missing. I left him to his observations.

* * *

'I appear for Ms. Suzanne Bell, My Lord,' announced her Senior Counsel in his Cork accent. She made her voluptuous way to the witness box which was to be her stage for the next hour or so. I do not think there was a movement of that too-short journey that was missed by anyone in Court. She settled herself in the box. The members of the jury (this was one of the last personal injuries cases to be tried before a jury) settled in also, the men taking their civic duty a bit more seriously than the women.

'Ms. Bell, do you remember the evening of 10th December 1990? Or, more precisely, the early hours of the following morning?'

'I do,' she replied, crossing her legs.

'Where were you at the time and what were you doing?'

'I was in "Rollers" night-club as usual. I was manageress there and was on duty every night except Monday, from ten o'clock until anytime between three and six. Essentially, what I did was supervise. I saw that everyone was enjoying themselves, attended to any complaints and, if it was very busy, helped the waitresses to serve the drinks.'

'For the benefit of the members of the jury and, of course, His Lordship, who may not be familiar with "Rollers" or indeed any night-club, could you please describe what goes on there?'

Suzanne adjusted her collar before answering. ' "Rollers" is an upmarket night-club where members come to enjoy themselves, drinking and dancing. There is a small dance floor, loud music, girls clad in swim-suits who serve expensive wines and because it is a very popular spot in the heart of the city centre, it is usually quite crowded. The women tend to be in their thirties, the men more forties or fifties.' I could see His Lordship making mental notes.

Her Senior Counsel continued, 'I think it was about two in the morning when something unusual happened? Could you tell the Judge and jury about that, nice and slowly and in your own words? Make sure that the gentleman in the farthest corner of the jury box can hear you.' A totally unnecessary instruction since there was not the slightest danger of anyone missing a single action or syllable, so rapt was the Court's attention.

Court 3 is a splendid room, high-ceilinged and spacious. It befits the pursuit of justice and, in particular, Ms. Bell's pursuit. It can accommodate a large number of people, witnesses and interested spectators alike. Normally, there would not be many people in Court for a personal injuries action. Those directly involved, of course, as well as an odd barrister or solicitor hiding for a moment, a student or two, maybe a couple of court-watchers if it is raining (on fine days, they go to the zoo).

Today was different. It could have been a sensational murder or, at least, a defamation with a prominent politician or a celebrity from RTE. Word had got around and the Court was beginning to swell. Ms. Bell was too, as she rose to her pretty feet. Had Salome herself been in the witness box, she could not have caused such a stir. From her pulpit, she explained, almost apologetically, that it might be easier to demonstrate what she had to say. Not a dissenting voice.

She began by explaining that it was a busy Saturday night and she was run off her feet. She couldn't remember the precise hour when the accident happened, but it was between two and three in the morning. She was attending to a party of ten or so who had just arrived. They had ordered three bottles of Chateau Neuf du Pape and she had placed them on the table. She had no difficulty opening the first two bottles. She was on the third. With this, her method evidence took over. In sporting parlance, she 'talked us through it'. But not before she shifted her stance, achieving the precise angle at which everybody in Court, particularly the Judge and the man in the farthest corner of the jury box, could see her to the best advantage.

'I picked up the last bottle of Chateau Neuf. I remember that "Rhythm is a Dancer" was playing at the time. I covered the top of the wine bottle with the opener. I turned the handle of the opener so that the screw would twist its way into the cork. When the screw had penetrated as far as it could, I applied pressure to the two wings of the opener which usually would result in the smooth withdrawal of the cork from the bottle. But not this time. I applied a little more pressure, but still the cork would not budge. I was anxious not to break the cork.'

At this point she bent her body ever so slightly, simultaneously placing the imaginary bottle between her not-so imaginary thighs. Undivided attention was taking on a new meaning.

'Holding the bottle in this way with my left hand, I began to pull on the bottle-opener with my right. Gently at first and then with greater force. I was having great difficulty in removing the cork. I decided on one final effort before going for another bottle. With that final pull, I felt the cork stir in the neck of the bottle. That gave me heart and I carried on pulling until eventually the cork was released. Unfortunately, the release of the cork was followed by a great flow of wine onto the Paul Costelloe dress of the host's partner. The eventual removal of the cork was so sudden and took me so by surprise that my neck jerked forwards and back causing a severe dart of pain.'

With this, an exquisite pain went right around the courtroom like a Mexican wave. By now, Mr. Justice Fleming was almost sitting on the Bench, such was his concern for this courageous plaintiff. He had the presence of mind to ask her to repeat the demonstration for the transcript. At this stage, the stenographer was tapping out the notes with his toes.

'The pain came and went. For the next few moments, I was so concerned about the dress that I didn't think further about my neck. It wasn't until I was home in bed that I became aware of my neck again. I didn't sleep that night.' With that, she resumed her seat to a rapturous silence.

She went on to deal with the following week and how she had battled on until a week later she had to submit and report the accident. From that time she had not been able to resume her highly paid job at 'Rollers'.

* * *

There was considerably less interest in Henry's elevation to his articulate feet. The task he faced was of Himalayan proportions. Ms. Bell's performance, for that is what it was, had been nothing short of consummate. Should she win her case, she should set up a training school for expert witnesses. A look here, a look there. In one moment, the coyness of a princess; in the next, the impishness of a truant schoolgirl. For one answer, her voice reached every corner of the Court; for the next, the Court would have to strain to the edge of its seat to catch every mellifluous syllable. Was she an actress conveying great innocence or an innocent conveying great acting? She crossed and recrossed her legs with a frequency and exposure that belied her convent education. It was a long time since she put a telephone book between her and the fellow on whose lap she was sitting. She played with her prey and her prey enjoyed the play. In short, it was the mother of all seductions.

Cross-examination of Ms. Bell called for a deftness of touch, a delicacy of footwork, that I was not sure Henry possessed. This was not a moment for a footrush or a garryowen. What was called for was a slip up the wing and over the line before anyone even knew you had the ball.

There would be no point in 'I must put it to you that you are lying or malingering or exaggerating'. It would be necessary, in an unfortunate phrase, to get in under her, to join her and flirt with her and ultimately to unmask her, so that before she knew it herself her audience would spot that there was more to this sweetness and light than appeared at first sight.

Humourless, monogamous Henry, full of EU Law and *de bene esse*, came out of his corner. What was called for was advocacy at its most elegant. I could think of one or two of Henry's colleagues who had it. Did Henry? I was about to find out.

'My Lord, before I commence my cross-examination, I would ask you to direct Ms. Bell to sit properly in the witness box. It may not be obvious to Your Lordship, but she is sitting in such a way as to distract me from my task.'

If ever a contribution was calculated to lose a jury, this was it. A silent chorus of disapproval rang around the Court. His Lordship was fully aware of Henry's problem because, notwithstanding the angle and the panelling, His Lordship had been able to secure himself a full view of the witness, as was his obligation under the Constitution, albeit at the risk of his own personal whiplash, a risk he seemed happy to take.

Furthermore, His Lordship knew well that Henry's application was premised on an untruth. There was about as much likelihood of Henry being distracted by Ms. Bell's legs as there was of Judge Fleming being interested in her IQ. Henry would likely find a judgment of the European Court more exciting.

'Really, Mr. Fitzmartin, I do not think I have any jurisdiction over how a witness sits in the witness box, as long as she is showing respect for the Court. I do not see any evidence of disrespect for the Court on Ms. Bell's part. In fact, the evidence is all to the contrary. I think she is an adornment.'

His Lordship looked towards the jury. The jury nodded approvingly.

'If you wish to persist in your application, you will have to refer me to some authority on the matter because, really, Mr. Fitzmartin, this is quite an unusual application.'

Henry decided to concede the first point. 'Very well, My Lord.'

An inauspicious start. He paused to assemble his first question and, as if to help him on his way, Ms. Bell achieved, quite effortlessly, a double leg-over. The right leg went across the left thigh in the conventional manner, to be followed by a tucking in of the right foot behind the left calf. The jury awarded her 9.9 for this, but His Lordship quickly overruled them and gave her a 10. As if to confirm the authenticity of his application, Henry's pause lengthened.

★ ★ ★

Cross-examination began and continued without any success, save in regard to length. The jury was grateful to Henry for keeping Ms. Bell in the box for as long as was forensically possible. Had it been any other witness, Henry would have been asked by His Lordship, normally quite an impatient arbiter, if it was really necessary to go over all this for the fifth time. There was as little sign of impatience on the Judge's part as there was an end to Henry's cross-examination.

From time to time, Arnold scribbled furiously and then, without waiting for one of the several lulls in cross-examination, which Henry used to construct his next forensic ace, Arnold, without raising his head, simply stuck out his hand with the projecting note. His hand might stay suspended there for some time until, at last, Henry would take the note and either crumple it immediately in his palm and then discard it or, occasionally, read it and bend down towards Arnold for an eternity of a consultation before eventually crumpling and discarding it. Either way, the end result as far as the note was concerned was the same. And Arnold, undeterred, went onto his next message.

Much to the delight of his colleague from the South, Henry had, in the course of his cross-examination, given the Plaintiff countless opportunities to satisfy the jury of her genuineness and of the severity of her continuing symptoms. He decided that she should have one last chance to increase her damages.

Sensing that Henry was entering the home straight, but without any certainty thereof, I heard him ask, 'Ms. Bell, one final question. I would like to put it to you and it is only fair to you to say that the orthopaedic surgeon who will be giving evidence on behalf of the Defence will say and you are entitled to an opportunity to rebut it, namely, that for some time you have recovered from your injuries and have been without symptom or disability? In short, Ms. Bell, that you are, not to put a tooth in it, exaggerating? What do you say to that?'

Before she had a chance to say anything, our friend from Cork was on his feet.

'My Lord, I don't like to interrupt my friend's cross-examination, but that does seem to be a number of questions wrapped up in one.'

'I agree entirely, but I think that Ms. Bell is well able to look after herself.'

Ms. Bell, assembling herself for her last routine, expanded and expounded and eventually confirmed His Lordship's confidence in her: 'Mr. Fitzmartin, I am afraid that I have to disagree with you and your orthopaedic surgeon. I have not had a pain-free day since this accident, so much so that in recent times I have been getting quite depressed. I was sent to a psychiatrist and he has me on medication and wants to see me once a month for the moment.'

'My Lord, I protest. This is the first we have heard of a psychiatric dimension to the Plaintiff's injuries. There is nothing about this in the pleadings. It wasn't mentioned by my friend in opening. Ms. Bell didn't say anything about it in her direct evidence.'

'But, Mr. Fitzmartin, it has arisen in the course of cross-examination. In reply to one of your own questions.'

'But, My Lord, it is too late in the day for this sort of evidence to be introduced. I would have to ask Your Lordship for an adjournment so that the Plaintiff could be examined by a psychiatrist on behalf of the Defendant.'

'Mr. Fitzmartin, I repeat that you cannot complain about evidence that is given in answer to your questions. I will not adjourn the case. Carry on, Ms. Bell.'

'Thank you, My Lord. Now, what was I saying?'

'You were telling the members of the jury that you hadn't a pain-free day since the accident, Ms. Bell,' assisted His Lordship before resuming his note-taking.

'Thank you again, My Lord. Yes. In fact, the slightest activity sets off the pain. For example, do you see what His Lordship is doing at the moment? (If Judges could purr – Mr. Justice Fleming looked up with a smile the width of the Four Courts as if to say, 'Who? Me?') Writing! I can't do that for more than a few minutes at a time. If I am writing a letter, I will develop a very severe pain in my neck after a very short time and I will have to go and lie down.' Another £10,000 goes onto Mr. Wilkinson's bill.

'Thank you, Ms. Bell.'

'Thank you, Mr. Fitzmartin.'

Ms. Bell left the witness box and carefully resumed her place on the touchline seats facing the jury. There was just time for a short witness before the lunch break. Mr. Bell must have been about fifteen years older than his wife. His function in the case was to set the domestic scene and to tell the jury how the accident had affected his wife on a day-to-day basis. Like most husbands, he was a perfect foil to his wife. Calm and colourless. In addition to which he was in an unique position to tell the jury about his wife's condition, not simply because he was her husband but because since he had taken early retirement as a result of a heart attack some years earlier he was at home most of the time, so he knew exactly how his wife was progressing. He had even given up his golf.

Henry, too, had had a heart attack but he did not give up his golf nor did he take early retirement. It may have been because of this or it may have been because of his singular lack of success in cross-examining Ms. Bell, but Henry seemed to forget momentarily that it didn't matter how much time Mr. Bell spent around the house or how he occupied his day or indeed if he was committing perjury, as Mr. Bell was not the Plaintiff.

Notwithstanding, Henry is intent on making some inroads into Mr. Bell's evidence. 'Mr. Bell, you have told us that you spend most of your day at your home in Rathmines. How do you pass the time?'

'Mr. Fitzmartin, I have always enjoyed literature and I have set myself a project of re-reading the classics.'

Making no effort to disguise his irritation with this dilettante and thinking of the hours that he puts in poring over briefs while Mr. Bell is poring over the classics, Henry comments, 'Lucky you. I would love to have time to re-read the classics.'

'This is all very interesting, Mr. Fitzmartin,' His Lordship interrupts, 'but I wonder if in your case would you be re-reading them?' Thus bringing to an end what was for Henry an unrewarding morning.

'Two o'clock, gentlemen?' announced, more than enquired, Judge Fleming.

'I wonder, My Lord, could you say 2.15? Ms. Bell has to collect her children from school.'

'Does that suit you, Mr. Fitzmartin?'

'May it please Your Lordship.'

* * *

I couldn't wait to get to my lunch table. One or two of my pals had never been to 'Rollers' and so did not know Suzanne. These few were more interested in the legal issues. How is she on liability? Was it not a case of *res ipsa loquitur*? What about foreseeability? And other mouth-watering questions from the academically minded at the table (little Henrys in the making).

The rest of my friends were more interested in my blow-by-blow account of Suzanne's evidence, every word and accompanying description of the opening of the bottle. Some of them knew her or thought they knew her. Was she the one with . . . or the one who . . .? She was and all. If there were any spare seats this morning, it was an all-ticket affair this afternoon.

In fact, the afternoon got off to a dull start. The Plaintiff completed her case, engineer, doctors, vocational assessor, actuary. By the time the vocational assessor had finished his evidence, one might have been forgiven for wondering if the Plaintiff was fit enough to collect her disability allowance. If she did not appear so disabled in the witness box, then presumably this was one of her better days. It was difficult to visualise this particular Plaintiff as an inner-city carpark attendant, but certainly the £150,000 that would have settled this case at eleven o'clock this morning was beginning to look less unrealistic.

The afternoon lulled on. We went into evidence. I studied the jury as our witnesses appeared. The only member of the jury who was not staring across at the Plaintiff as if hypnotised was asleep. Still, our main card was yet to be played. The private investigator.

I knew just how important the PI was to our case. Arnold had told me that Mr. Wilkinson was normally a very reasonable Claims Manager. Reasonable in his attitude to settlements. He took an economic point-of-view. Bought off risks. It wasn't a question of fighting everything to the death regardless of the consequences. But the one thing he couldn't take was fraud. When it came to fraud, he had a blind spot. Reason went out the window. In this case, from the beginning there was ground for suspicion. Mr. Wilkinson kept a close eye on developments. He was going to make the decision in the end.

The medical report endorsed his preliminary view that maybe he was being codded. But the PI's report and photographs convinced him. He would offer the value of the case on the basis of our medical evidence and after that the case could fight. And that is exactly what happened.

If I knew how important this witness was to our case, I also knew how wrong a PI's evidence could go. Most judges were not enamoured with private investigators. I suppose it's the old Irish thing about the informer. Only over lunch my pals were telling me of two cases where the PI went horribly wrong. Both cases involved churches. The first was where the Plaintiff was alleging that he could not bend or lift, and the PI had a video of him carrying his wife's coffin down the aisle to the hearse. The second case was a Plaintiff who insisted on a severe limp and a walking-stick. He was caught giving his daughter away, neither limp nor stick in sight as he led her up the aisle in his best military march. In both cases, the PI was unceremoniously dumped. Happily, our PI's evidence was less controversial.

I got the fright of my life when, at about 3.30, Henry turned to me and asked, 'Would you like to take the next witness?' If he took me by surprise earlier (at the consultation when he asked me, 'What do you think?'), it was nothing to the surprise I was now feeling. The only thing that was clear was that there was no-one else to whom the question could have been addressed.

I don't know why but what immediately occurred to me was a friend's account of how he dealt with an identical predicament, albeit a little earlier in what we were now beginning to refer to as our careers. He fled. Quite simply, he fled. Between the moment when his Senior turned around and issued the invitation and the moment when he was expected to soar to his ambitious feet, he left Court. To this day, he does not know if the invitation was serious. Did his Senior even know the stir he caused? Or, as the appointed moment lengthened into a protracted silence, did the Judge look down on Senior wondering why he was not bestirring himself, while Senior, sedentary and unconscious of the vacuum behind him, wondered why His Lordship seemed perplexed.

This was the stuff that dreams were made of. Many the sleep that was induced by a sterling cross-examination that catapults me to fame and fortune. In current jargon, this was a window of opportunity. It would not be unduly pessimistic or disloyal of me to say that this case was not running too well from Mr. Wilkinson's point of view. Even he must see that. If the jury was, by its enforced silence, more discreet than His Lordship, it was safe to say that the Plaintiff was fighting a downhill battle. It fell to me to turn the tide. Never having taken a witness in the High Court before, indeed never having been in the High Court before, you could say that I was relatively inexperienced. No. On reflection, you could drop the 'relatively'. I was inexperienced.

Really, there was no time for these musings. I rose to my nervous feet.

★ ★ ★

'Come up, Mr. Smith.' (This was our star witness, the PI.)

For one moment, I wondered could this be the most treacherous of hospital passes. Perhaps after all, Henry was more streetwise than I gave him credit for. As quickly as the thought came, it vanished and I heard myself ask, 'I think, Mr. Smith, you were asked by my solicitor to watch Ms. Bell on behalf of the Defendant in this case? And, in particular, with the assistance of camera and video to see if you could come up with evidence that might be useful to the Defendant in the defence of this action?'

'That is correct,' replied Mr. Smith.

'Were you told that Ms. Bell was alleging a serious neck injury requiring constant use of her collar and that she was unable to engage in any activity that required movement of her neck?'

'I was.'

'Did you, in fact, watch Ms. Bell and take photographs of her and did you video her?'

'I did. I watched her and took photographs and videoed her. For reasons that will become clear, I am no longer in possession of this video.' (This was not going too badly, I thought to myself.)

'Now Mr. Smith, will you tell the Ladies and Gentlemen of the jury what you saw?'

'Well, on 31st May 1994, at about 8am, I positioned my vehicle at a discreet distance from Ms. Bell's house which, as you know, is situated in a cul-de-sac in Rathmines. It wasn't difficult on the first day, but the fact that she lived in a cul-de-sac was going to make observing her quite awkward thereafter. In any event, on that first morning there was no sign of any movement. At about 11am, I decided to call to the house to see if she was there. She answered the door and I talked to her on a pretext. I was able to confirm that she was the Plaintiff in this action and I now confirm that the lady I spoke to is the same person as gave evidence in Court here this morning. We spoke briefly and I left.'

'Did you notice anything about her?'

'What do you mean?'

'Well, did you notice anything about her dress?' I knew that, whatever about a greater informality in the Circuit Court, I would not get away with a leading question in the High Court.

Unfortunately, Mr. Smith was a little slow on the uptake. 'Oh yes, her dress. Well, actually, I thought it was a very pretty dress.' The jury and everyone else in Court giggled. They could sense a breakdown in communication. I was, you might say, temporarily out of contact with my witness.

Beware the helpful Judge. 'Mr. McNamara, why don't you try asking Mr. Smith the question you want to ask him?'

'Thank you, My Lord. Mr. Smith, did you notice whether or not Ms. Bell was wearing a cervical collar?'

'Oh, is that what you're getting at, Mr. McNamara? No, she was definitely not wearing a cervical collar.' (Thank God for that.)

'Please continue with your evidence, Mr. Smith.'

'I attended at Ms. Bell's home on a number of other occasions for the purpose of observing her. These attendances did not yield much information except that on a few occasions she left by car. She drove without difficulty and did not have any problem entering or leaving the car. On one occasion, she carried a television set out of the house and loaded it into the boot of her vehicle. I came to the conclusion that, more than likely, she was bringing it to the shop for repairs. I decided to follow her. Unfortunately, I had to let her out of the cul-de-sac before I could turn my vehicle and in doing so, I was delayed. I caught up with her at the traffic lights at Belgrave Square. She was driving a red BMW. It was only when the lights turned to green and the vehicles moved off that I noticed that, by extraordinary coincidence, there was a second red BMW. One went left towards

Rathmines. The other right towards Ranelagh. Unfortunately, I followed the wrong red BMW. I had no option but to discontinue my observations.'

Emboldened by my earlier experience, I asked straight out, 'Mr. Smith, did you happen to notice if Ms. Bell was wearing a collar on any of the occasions on which you observed her?'

'Mr. McNamara!' The honeymoon was over. 'Really, you should know better than that. I allowed it the first time, but I cannot permit this examination-in-chief to be conducted on the basis of leading questions. This is, after all, the High Court. The rules of evidence may not be observed in the Courts in which you normally practice, but please observe them in my Court.' Mr. Justice Fleming looked sternly towards the jury.

'Mr. Smith, did you notice anything about the Plaintiff on these occasions when you observed her? I mean, what was she wearing or not wearing?' I enquired, afraid to look at His Lordship.

'Her collar, My Lord, she was not wearing her collar on any of these occasions,' Mr. Smith replied, jumping back on the bandwagon.

'May I bring you on now to the afternoon of Saturday, 21st June 1994? I think you took up your position again on that afternoon. Is that right?'

'Yes, it is. It was a gorgeous summer's day. I remember it well. We were in the middle of a heat wave. The men were strolling shirtless around the park. Girls in the shortest of skirts were spreading themselves on the grass. It was certainly not a day for working, especially a Saturday.'

'Mr. Smith, would you mind coming to the point?'

'Sorry, My Lord, I was just painting the picture.'

'Mr. Smith, if you wouldn't mind confining yourself to the evidence that might be relevant to the case and keeping the painting for your spare time. Now, you were about to tell us what happened on this heavenly Saturday.'

'Yes, My Lord. Sorry, My Lord. The first thing I noticed was that Ms. Bell's hall door was open and that Mr. and Mrs. Bell were in the front garden. There is no rear garden. The next thing I noticed is that they were rather curiously dressed. Ms. Bell was dressed in nun's apparel, the old traditional style. Long flow of black and white with wimple and veil. She was trying to attach a rosary beads. Nearby, Mr.

Bell in all the splendour of a pre–Vatican II Bishop. It was only as Ms. Bell turned to go up the steps to her hall door that I noticed that this was no conventional nun. There was no back to her outfit. The only concession to modesty was a black bra and panties. I was able to take some photographs.'

My learned friend with the Cork accent was quick to his southern feet. 'My Lord, I am not quite sure where this is leading. Of what possible relevance can photographs of my client in nun's garb be?'

I was pleased with my speed off the mark. 'Was she wearing a collar, Mr. Smith?'

'No.'

'There, My Lord. There's the relevance, Photographs of the Plaintiff who has sworn to Your Lordship that she has to wear a collar all the time without the very collar. That's the relevance, My Lord.'

'Very well, Mr. McNamara, I'll allow the photographs. There may well be an innocent explanation for not wearing the collar at that moment. It was after all, on Mr. Smith's evidence, a very hot day. I'll allow them *de bene esse*, as your leader would say.'

A nod of acknowledgment from Henry. I felt that there was an unseemly haste, led by His Lordship, about the manner in which the photographs were grabbed. The absence of a collar was not the only thing they confirmed. It seemed to take a little longer than usual for everyone to peruse them.

Eventually, Mr. Smith resumed. 'I engaged Mr. Bell in conversation and before I left ascertained that he and his wife were going to a midsummer fancy-dress barbecue in their tennis club. Dancing from eight to late to Johnny and the Jets.'

I could sense a little discomfort on the Bench. Notwithstanding judicial obstruction, Mr. Smith was making a little headway. His Lordship did not know what was coming, but he realised that damage, maybe considerable damage, could be done to his, or rather, Ms. Bell's case. He decided to become even more interventionist.

'What did you do next, Mr. Smith?' I explored. 'I decided to attend the barbecue.' 'And did you attend?' 'I did.'

Fleming J saw his chance. 'What time did you arrive, Mr. Smith?' 'About ten o'clock, My Lord.' 'And did you go alone?' 'No, My Lord, I went with my partner.' 'Did you have any trouble getting in?' 'No, by that time everyone was enjoying themselves and the security was quite relaxed.' 'What did you do once you got in?' 'We mingled.' 'Mingled, Mr. Smith? Tell the members of the jury how you mingled.'

'Well,' Mr Smith warmed to his subject, 'the first thing we did was to get something to eat. Then we split up and moved around. It was a while before I found Ms. Bell. Obviously, from her costume there was no difficulty identifying her, but there were a lot of guests and it was sometime before I found her. After a while we joined forces again. My partner began videoing. By now everyone was in good form and photographs were being taken and one or two others were videoing. All the time Ms. Bell was causing quite a stir in her nun's outfit.'

Then, as if the question had just occurred to him, though it was quite clear to me that he had been building up to it, His Lordship asked, 'And you, Mr. Smith, and your partner, were you not a bit conspicuous at this fancy-dress, strolling around with your video camera?' 'No, My Lord.' 'And why was that, Mr. Smith? Did you dress up as well?' 'I did, My Lord.' 'And your partner, did she dress up also?' 'He, My Lord.' 'Well, did he dress up?' 'He did, My Lord.'

'Now, Mr. Smith, tell the Ladies and Gentlemen of the jury how did you dress up?' 'Well, My Lord, like everyone else, in fancy-dress.' (No, Mr. Smith, I thought to myself, don't try to be clever with His Lordship. Just answer the question.) 'There's no need to be clever, Mr. Smith, just answer the question. I'm sure the jury is very curious to know how you and your friend were dressed for the fancy-dress.'

After a pause, 'Clowns, My Lord.'

'Clowns, Mr. Smith?'

'Yes, My Lord.'

'Both of you, Mr. Smith?'

'I'm afraid so, My Lord.'

'You and your friend attended this barbecue with your videos dressed up as clowns, Mr. Smith?'

'That's right, My Lord.'

Whereupon the Court dissolved in laughter. Maureen Potter was never as good as this. You could bring this show around the country. Junior for the Plaintiff had to leave Court. Even His Lordship, who had masterminded the entire scene, couldn't contain himself. I couldn't see my so-called friends around the courtroom, but I could sense them. They were not missing a word of it.

Having regard to the way the wind was blowing before ever Mr. Smith got into the box, he had to be spectacularly good to turn the tide. As things turned out, through no fault of his own, he was spectacularly bad. His Lordship had succeeded in laughing him out of Court.

It was sometime before the Court regained its composure and it was possible to resume. But resume we did, after a fashion. I fumbled on as best I could. Neither Judge nor jury was paying the slightest attention to me and still less to Mr. Smith. I just wanted the entire shambles to end.

I would say that I was the only one in Court to hear Mr. Smith's account of the remainder of the barbecue. How Ms. Bell had danced her pretty legs off and what there was of her costume until the early hours of that midsummer dawn. How Clouseau and sidekick had videoed the entire party until they were eventually copped about two o'clock. They were encouraged out onto one of the more remote tennis courts where, at a remove from courting couples, they were asked, in a most threatening manner, their business. Very quickly, the video camera was confiscated and they were sent on their hapless way.

The evidence cast a dark shadow over the credibility of Ms. Bell. Or, at least, it would have had it been heard. But no-one heard a word of it. Or, if they did, no-one heeded it. The damage had been done. Bring on the clowns.

Forlornly I asked, 'Mr. Smith, during the entire evening, was there sight of a collar?' I could ask any leading question I cared to at this stage.

'None.'

I resumed my seat where I buried my face in my hands. Cross-examination was as short as it was superfluous.

'Four o'clock, Gentlemen. Shall we say eleven tomorrow morning?'

★ ★ ★

I couldn't get to the sanctuary of the tea-room quickly enough. I was safe there from Arnold and Mr. Wilkinson. As I saw it, my career was in tatters. My debut in the High Court and I couldn't jump the first hurdle. In front of a capacity crowd into the bargain. I was badly in need of some friendly therapy. I joined my friends. They were talking about the case all right, but not in a manner that was likely to give me any solace. Puerile references to Ms. Bell's anatomy. Peels of laughter as the evidence was recalled: 'And what were you dressed up as, Fleming asked . . . A clown, replied Mr. Smith'. And the entire table resounded. Others joined in, attracted by the story.

I arrived needing attention and soothing words. As the tale grew out of all proportions, I was happy to be left alone. After a suitable interval, I slunk off unnoticed.

It was all over bar the shouting. I had a most uncomfortable night. No matter what way I turned the case and my participation in it, it came out a disaster. My sleep was invaded by nuns and clowns and hysterical laughter. I awoke exhausted, not knowing how to face the day. For face it I must.

Henry and his opposite number harangued the jury. I don't blame Henry for not being able to come up with something overnight that might deflect them from their intended course of awarding massive damages. Even if he had, its effect would have been utterly undone by Mr. Justice Fleming's one-sided charge to the jury. On the one or two occasions that His Lordship attempted to summarise the evidence to them in a manner that bore some semblance of neutrality (at least as far as language was concerned), his delivery was couched in such silent signals, wrapped in such raised eyebrows, as to leave the twelve good persons and true in no reasonable doubt as to the Judge's real meaning.

And so it came to pass. Shortly before lunch. The jury returned for one last lustful look at Sister Suzanne before crowning her with their award, which greatly exceeded her expectations. There was nothing silent about the celebration that began on the Plaintiff's side of the Court even before Mr. Justice Fleming left the Bench. It was as much as one could do to assemble one's papers and retreat as quickly as possible. There was no difficulty about anonymity. There was plenty of that.

As I left the Court, I heard the Plaintiff's solicitor on her mobile making a reservation for lunch at the 'Lord Edward'. I made a mental note to enter *Bell v. Rollers* with *DPP v. Wilkinson* in my record of cases under the letter 'N' – for nightmare.

I turned towards the wilderness. I knew the way.

★ ★ ★

6

The Belleville National

One of the hallowed traditions – in fact *the* hallowed tradition – of the Bar is the pursuit of money. Nothing should be allowed to come between the individual barrister and the fulfilment of his or her quest for fortune. Like all worthwhile traditions in Irish history, it is too sacred to be written down. Instead, enshrined indelibly in each barrister's memory, it is passed from generation to generation by word of mouth. In fact, the more enlightened recruits to the Law Library do not even have to be taught this tradition. It is part of what they are.

From time to time, a competing philosophy raises its ugly head and it is this: no person should be denied access to the Courts for lack of funds. It can be seen immediately that these two philosophies are mutually exclusive. Certainly, they cannot cohabit on any long–term basis. At best, the first can have a from–time–to–time flirtation with the second. In this way, they seek to accommodate one another.

Since the introduction of legal aid in criminal and matrimonial cases, the principal manifestation of what is arguably the more noble of the two philosophies is on the civil side in relation to personal injury cases. Day-in day-out, cases of varying degrees of spuriosity are launched by barristers and solicitors on a 'no foal, no fee' basis. In this way, the claims of 'tinker, tailor, soldier, sailor, (rich man?), poor man, beggar man, thief', which otherwise would never see the light of Court, are litigated and the 'small man' declared entitled to damages or not as the case may be. If he succeeds, then the legal team will share in that success and will be rewarded for its endeavours. If not, the concept of swings and roundabouts will be invoked and beidh lá eile.

Twinned with this vocation to make money at all costs is this dimly lit ideal, namely, to look after the man in the Clapham omnibus if he cannot afford your fare. This duty weighs heavily. It is incumbent on all barristers, young and old, successful and less so, to take on his or her fair share of this work. Invariably, of course, the brunt of the burden falls on the 'young' and the 'less so'. As in all things relating to the law, the test is reasonableness. The obligation is not to take on every free-loader. The obligation does not mean that your entire practice should be run on this basis. I sometimes felt that my practice had misinterpreted the obligation.

Arnold had what I call a 'referred social conscience'. He referred it to me. He had an expanding personal injury practice. As much of it as possible he would settle as early as possible, directly with the insurance company and without the assistance of Counsel. This was the most profitable course from his point of view. He would only engage Counsel as a last resort and at the last moment.

For Court he had three teams. The 'A' team handled the big cases. The 'B' team handled the not-so-big, but safe cases. The 'C' team got the 'iffy' and the 'very iffy' cases where, if you won, the damages would be small but, in fact, any talk of damages would be a bonus because you were unlikely to get that far. This was where Arnold's referred social conscience comes in, coinciding with my recent elevation to his 'C' team. There was not much competition for places.

I would not like you to get the idea that there was anything even remotely altruistic about my willingness to do these cases for nothing. It was merely an unhappy coincidence between having nothing at all to do and the irrational hope that somehow, out of all this imposed selflessness, some selfish benefit might accrue. Somehow.

I should have mentioned that even the 'iffy' cases have their own internal hierarchy. There are the 'iffy' cases which Arnold will attend and the even 'iffier' ones where he will send Samantha, his secretary, along. Arnold imposes this discipline on his social conscience. If the case is hopeless, he will attend in person. If the case is hopeless and unwinnable, Samantha is despatched and Arnold will go elsewhere and close a sale. In this way, the practice of J. Arnold O'Reilly & Co. hovers on the south side of solvency.

* * *

The later the phone call the evening before, the 'iffier' the case. So when the phone went at 10.25 this particular evening, it was no surprise. (At that moment, I was heavily into a lightly blue movie while feeding our eighteen-month-old twins. My twelve-month-old wife was out at a Circuit dinner and wasn't expected in until the early hours. How things have changed.) By now I didn't expect an apology for the lateness of the call.

'Is that you, Dermot?' (Who else?) 'Neither Kelly nor Moore are free tomorrow. You're in. (Note the assumption that I am available.) 9.25 as usual. Samantha will be down. (*That* 'iffy' obviously.) She'll have the papers. Court 7. Judge Foley.' (Judge Foley sits in Court 8, but no matter.)

All the information I'll ever need. Certainly all the information I'll ever get. Kelly, Moore and Arnold out. Samantha in. Need any more be said about the chances of success? Of course, there will be no-one there at 9.25 and it would be a first if Samantha's file was less skimpy than her skirt. It's a very brief phone call, but it encompasses a lot of information, if somewhat sketchy on details of the actual case.

Let me tell you about Samantha. She is tall with long legs and always sports a mini-skirt. Inevitably blond. The rest of us breathe to stay alive. Samantha chews gum. I have never actually seen her blow a bubble, but she looks as if she is on a constant alert to do so. She may have chewed gum for Ireland. She cannot walk ten yards without plugging herself in to her Walkman, so that while there is no certainty about engaging her attention when she is with you, there is no means of communication once she has wired herself up to 65 IQ or whatever local station is on offer. In the journey from Gardiner Street, she generates more litigation than any courier with her weaving, unhearing, in and out of potential plaintiffs.

Is it necessary to add that she has not the slightest interest in the case? And even less in me. I still have to discover what precise service she provides for Arnold that makes her worthy of her pay packet. True to Arnold's word, she will have papers with her and those that she gives to me I will call a Brief and the remainder she will retain herself. It would be a mistake to assume that because she holds on to some of the papers she has any familiarity with their contents. (Once or twice, impelled by that assumption, I have enquired about some matters, the answers to which might have appeared on the retained papers. Without any articulation whatever, Samantha simply handed me the file and carried on chewing.) If I turn my head for a moment, the head-phones are back on and we are airborne again.

It is just as well she is not the Plaintiff because she is not exactly Judge Foley's cup of tea. Not even in Judge Foley's obituary will it be said that he was a man of the people. A snob by birth and conviction, he made no attempt to conceal it. Quite the reverse. He paraded it. He was the only person I ever knew whose passion was polo, though it had been a decade or two since he had graced the Phoenix Park himself.

Before his elevation to the Bench, he had enjoyed a large reputation and practice in the commercial field. Being a man of independent means (his father made a small fortune in ladies' underwear), he did not need a practice, but he liked his work and was good at it. Coming from that side of the Court, it is unlikely that he ever heard of the 'no foal, no fee' expression other than in an equine context. If he had ever done a personal injuries case, no-one remembered. Such cases should not be allowed to take up the valuable time of the Court, but should be consigned to a quasi-judicial tribunal, would have been his view. On the Bench, Judge Foley treated these cases accordingly.

It was a surprise when he took the Circuit Court. He had been widely tipped for a High Court position. Intellectually he was up to it and his subscription was up to date. It was felt that a recent heart condition might be the explanation.

★ ★ ★

As usual I am on time – 9.25. As usual Samantha is not. Punctuality isn't a hallmark of Arnold's office. I hang around the Library door until she arrives.

There is no difficulty whiling away the time here, no danger of dying from loneliness. The nerve centre of the Library, ever a hive of activity and inactivity, the threshold of this great room with its ceilings as high as Nelson's Pillar and its shelved walls packed with Court dramas of yesteryear. Not exactly best-sellers, even in their day, but still pursued and perused from time to time by a determined colleague fingering, from the top of a ladder, each dusty tome until at last he finds '*Boyle v. Ferguson* [1911] 2 I.R. 489'.

It is from here that we are paged. The briefing solicitor presents himself at the horseshoe-shaped reception desk, where he furnishes his barrister's name to the Crier who then calls the name through a microphone that reaches every corner of the far-flung Library. The uninitiated cannot understand how, when so many names are being called at one time, each barrister can identify his or hers to the exclusion of all others. It is not so long since the names were sung out by Tommy without the assistance of modern technology, each name being invested by him with its own internal rhythm. Only a few years later, it is difficult to conceive of the entire Library being corralled in this way by one unaided human voice. In truth, an unique art.

Inside the Library, there is another reception desk where colleagues page one another and are paged for the phone. Barristers sweep by, heading for their desks or the Robing Room in one direction or Court in the other, barely stopping to tell the receptionists the number of the Court they are going to. From here, rows of benches, crowned with papers and books, unfold along the length of the Library like waves. Here, colleagues assemble to share the day-long gossip, the latest cross-examination, the latest 'Did you hear what Foley has done now?' There is no difficulty in passing the time of day, or indeed the day itself, in this cesspool of calumny and mirth.

On the fringe of this early morning congregation, I distract myself from Samantha's tardiness until eventually, at 10.15, gummed and head-phoned, she sails in, oblivious to any timetable. Apologising for unpunctuality is not a hallmark of Arnold's office either apparently.

Not one to stand on ceremony, Anto (the Plaintiff) is introduced to Dermot (that's me) and Dermot to Anto. And to Anto's father, Anto Senior, and Anto's girlfriend and Thomas (the witness). On first-name terms so soon, we are on our way to a lifelong friendship.

As kick-off is at 10.30, there will be no time for the consultation room, which in any event had not been booked because of the 'iffy' nature of the case. It transpires that Anto lives in Belleville and is unemployed. He hasn't done a day's work in the thirty years of his life to date, and if a role model of 2,000 years ago began his public life at thirty it is unlikely that Anto, even if he is aware of this, will follow suit. He is a fit, athletic-looking man of boyish looks who cannot attribute his unemployment to physical infirmity. A high forehead often suggests intelligence but not, I fear, in Anto's case. He sports the inevitable pony-tail, which will not endear him to Judge Foley who considers that such appendages are strictly for women and horses. A few questions and I realise that if it is ever a crime to be articulate, Anto need have no worries of a criminal record. His friend Thomas, altogether a darker-looking gentleman, answers all the questions for Anto, who looks to Thomas at all times for what might loosely be called inspiration. This poses a problem from the evidential point of view because they will not be allowed to give their evidence together and prompting from the well of the Court is frowned upon.

* * *

It was far from bluebell time in Belleville. The incident unfolded – it was a misty, drizzly December afternoon about 3.30. Anto had gone for a walk in the vast park near where he lived and, at the dramatic moment, was making his unemployed way home. He was alone. The only semblance of company was one or two joggers disappearing into the distance and some children finishing up their winter football game which they could hardly see. He was walking along a path at the time, a wall to his left. Suddenly, he was aware of being knocked against the wall with great force by he knew not what. He was rendered unconscious, only coming to in the ambulance. That was about as much as Anto could tell me of what happened and none of it proved negligence against anyone. Hopefully Thomas could throw some light on the incident. From the point of view of the injuries, Anto was lucky not to fracture his skull, but less lucky in relation to his elbow which he fractured severely and which would lead to arthritis.

Enter Thomas. Thomas of the grandstand view. Thomas and Anto had a nodding acquaintance. Thomas nodded to Anto and Anto to Thomas. They were not friends as such. Though they did live in back-to-back cul-de-sacs in the same housing estate. I asked if they ever had a drink together and was assured that they hadn't even been in the same pub at the same time. Accordingly, Thomas was as close to an independent witness as you could get.

This December afternoon, Thomas was in his bedroom. For no particular reason. At 3.30 exactly he looked out the window. For no particular reason. Do you have to have a reason for looking out your bedroom window at exactly 3.30 on a December afternoon?

He wasn't looking at anything in particular. Until suddenly, from out of the mist emerged a galloping horse. Just as suddenly, he realised that the horse was bearing down on this man who was walking in the same direction and wasn't aware of the horse. The collision was as inevitable as it was unexpected. Thomas immediately rushed to the man's assistance. He couldn't give any description of the animal.

It was on these facts that Anto had sued the County Council. There was no point in suing the real culprit who was the owner of the horse because even if the owner could be identified, which he couldn't, he would not be a mark for Anto's damages. Anto was injured through no fault of his own, so who do you sue? The County Council, of course. Who else? They own and maintain the park and Anto's case was that they shouldn't allow horses to stray within the park. There were wardens and rangers and bye-laws, and really it wasn't good enough. What if there had been children there at the time?

I asked how could the County Council be responsible for the wanderings of a single stray horse. Anto and his entourage were in no doubt. It wasn't a question of one stray horse, I was assured. Horses were a feature of animal life in the park. Owned either by tenants of the Council or by residents of the local halting site, the horses were kept in the park. As familiar to the park in Belleville as cows to Constable, I might have been told. And the Council did nothing about it.

I asked Samantha what she thought of our chances. 'Dunno. Wasn't listening,' she replied unhelpfully. I was on my own on this one.

* * *

Judge Foley differed from Samantha in a number of respects. One of these was punctuality. He sits at 10.30 on the dot and if you are not in Court when your case is called, it is struck out. It is extraordinary how quickly Judges forget what it was like being a barrister and the simultaneous demands in different Courts for your physical presence.

One minute to 10.30. I quickened my pace, passing on the trot scores of colleagues heading for the different Courts. The labyrinthine corridor leading to the staircase outside the Supreme Court was like

Henry Street on Christmas Eve and, of course, the greater your hurry the more crowded your passage. As I made my way up to Court 8 on the first floor wing of Gandon's great Temple of Justice, I did my best to assemble this newly acquired information into a winning package before Judge Foley. Along the corridor, as wide as the Liffey that runs parallel, past the chambers of Mr. Justice Fleming and Mr. Justice Moore. Who knows? Maybe one day, Mr. Justice McNamara? At the moment, however, plain untitled Dermot McNamara, BL, struggling with the facts of *Anto Mullen v. Dublin County Council*.

'Going on, My Lord.'

We're third on the List. There will be plenty of time for negotiation, which might be my best bet, I've decided. But with whom? The Junior Counsel who signed the defence has taken Silk, so the identity of his replacement will be important to Anto's prospects.

Defence Counsel tend to fall into a number of identifiable categories. 'Your client is a fraud', before you have said anything on his behalf, is one category. 'I'm doing my damnedest to get you money but you know Bloggs, he's a mean bastard' is another, lying, category. I was in dire need of the third, rarer, category: the one who wants to get you a few bob and be back in the Library for an early coffee.

Margaret Thompson, BL. I was about to discover a new category. Margaret was coming to the end of her highly successful career as a Junior and had been tipped to take Silk in recent calls. She was more often to be seen in the company of Seniors than her fellow-travellers at the Junior Bar. I thought it unlikely that she had ever set eyes on me before. A reliable topic over coffee was whether her beauty surpassed her intelligence or vice versa. It was a keen contest, with supporters evenly divided and both contestants finishing neck and neck. In truth, she was both and there are few indeed who are so divinely endowed on the double. In or out of her wig and gown, she was a joy to behold.

None of her attributes escaped her attention or were allowed to escape ours. Like an actress, she strutted them. Efficient, articulate and perhaps, most importantly, confident, she made the Court her own and her case as if it were the only one in the List. She didn't exactly talk to you; she addressed you. She also preferred to include in her conversation with you anyone even remotely within earshot, as if her words would be wasted if heard only by you. In this way, she made it difficult to build up the intimacy which successful negotiations sometimes call for.

Even before I had opened my mouth to Margaret, I felt a little inadequate, that in whatever discussions developed I would have the lower hand. The facts of my case did nothing to correct the imbalance.

'Margaret, I have to be quite frank with you. This is not the strongest case I've ever had,' doing my best to conceal from her the fact that it was not much weaker in truth than most of my cases.

Sometimes, in negotiation, a modicum of honesty pays. If you have a weak case, then settlement might be the preferred option from your client's point of view, in which case it would be a mistake to open too high. Confession to a certain weakness in your case can endear you to your opposite's sense of reasonableness with favourable result. Of course, it is essential to get the extent of that confession right: a little too much and your opposite number concludes, perhaps correctly, that you have no belief at all in your case, with disastrous consequences to your client.

'I have to agree with you, Dermot,' she replied with such self-righteous conviction as to suggest that were her information more widely known, the Plaintiff would not be here at all. (When you are acting for Plaintiffs in 'iffy' cases on any sort of regular basis, you grow accustomed to being patronised from the high moral ground occupied by insurance companies and other institutions and their symbiotic Counsel.)

'I think it is probably worth about £25,000, Margaret, but it is not without risks. On the one hand, Foley is not a good draw from our point of view and may not have much sympathy for the unemployed of Belleville. You, of course, will be arguing that the accident was entirely unforeseeable. Having said that, my Client is completely innocent and the Council ought to have been aware of the presence of stray horses. You have your risks too, Margaret.'

'Foreseeability may not be your biggest problem,' she replied enigmatically.

'What do you mean?'

'You'll see.' The bonding process was not going very well.

'Anyway, you can take it that I'm looking for £25,000, but will take less,' hoping that I was not giving too much away.

At least I had started the settlement ball rolling and had placed it firmly in her court, even if she had not given me much reason for believing that I would be going for an early coffee. I returned to Anto and company, a little puzzled. What did Margaret mean, 'Foreseeability may not be your biggest problem'? She clearly had some card up her pretty sleeve. Or was she bluffing? In the ordinary way, these veiled references would suggest a private investigator. But this was not really that sort of case. Anto had been knocked down by a horse and fractured his elbow. He was not making a mountain of his injuries and there was no claim for loss of earnings in view of his unemployment career. A PI would be more appropriate if, for example, he was claiming loss of earnings and they had photographs of him working. Having regard to the limitations of his claim, there wasn't a whole lot a PI could uncover.

I checked with Anto. 'Anything you haven't told me, Anto? Now's the time.'

'I've told you everything there is to tell.'

* * *

Time passed. Still no sign of us getting on. Nor any sign of Margaret coming back to me with the Defendant's response to my opening bid. So I decided to seek her out in the adjoining windowed alcove, where she and her witnesses were huddled in whispered tones.

'Any news, Margaret?' I enquired as if I wasn't really enquiring.

'What do you mean, Dermot?'

'Well I was looking for £25,000. Are you paying it?'

'No,' she replied, unable to find a more definite way of phrasing her refusal, at the same time returning to the alcove out of which she had not really stirred.

I wasn't ready for such outright rejection. Normally a demand, albeit inflated, is met by an offer, albeit depressed. And you take it from there. To-ing and fro-ing, giving and taking, until, eventually, agreement. But a down right 'No' wrongfooted me. Did she mean, 'No, I am not paying you £25,000' or 'No, I am not paying you anything'? I was about to find out.

'Well, is there any offer at all?' I asked with less nonchalance than before and hoping that my question might not be overheard by her team, from which I sought to disentangle her with a view to engaging in something that more closely resembled a conversation. I had to see if there was any possibility at all of settling this case.

She emerged from her corner and joined me at the far end of the corridor, away at last from her adoring audience. But not for long. Around the corner, in full regalia, led by his outrider, swept His Lordship, Mr. Justice Fleming. Not an opportunity to be passed up by His Lordship.

'Good morning, Margaret. As beautiful as ever.'

'Good morning, Judge. Why, thank you,' replies Margaret, bowing to just the right level of deference and, as she does, being eyed enthusiastically from top to toe by His admiring Lordship.

'How did you enjoy the Inns the other night?'

'Famously. I thought you made a very good speech.'

Margaret and Judge Fleming drop easily into the precise relationship that I require for my negotiation. They flatter each other. The Judge makes no attempt to conceal the fact that he enjoys the company of good-looking women and Margaret indulges his blatant sexism in the interests of her career and her vanity. I may as well not be there. As far as Mr. Justice Fleming is concerned, I am not.

When they disengage from their little coquetry, I am heard to say as the Judge passes, 'Good morning, Judge.'

'Oh yes, I see, quite, yes, good morning,' replies His Lordship, aware of my presence for the first time and making me feel something of a voyeur.

Margaret, such is her total composure, resumes our negotiations precisely where she had left off, almost as if the brief interlude with Judge Fleming was a figment of my imagination. 'No, Dermot, no offer, not a penny. My clients have taken a view on this one and I must say that I am inclined to agree with them.' 'Look, Margaret, I have already told you that I may have a problem on liability but . . .'

'It's not just liability. Did the accident happen at all?'

'What do you mean?'

'I've said too much already. If your client wants money, he'll have to get it from the Judge.'

I wasn't having much success with Margaret and clearly she was not going to put her pretty body out on my behalf. I decided to have one further go.

'You may not have it all your own way in there,' I said, playing the gender card in an undisguised reference to Foley's misogyny. Foley's reputation among my female colleagues was the opposite of Fleming's. If Fleming liked women passionately, Foley disliked them just as passionately. So much so that I suspect that something awful must have happened to him in the womb and he has been taking it out on women ever since. Very often with barristers their prejudices lie dormant or undetected while they are at the Bar and it is only when they are appointed to the Bench that they achieve full fruition. That cannot be said in Foley's case. His antipathy towards women was well heralded whilst at the Bar, but it undoubtedly scaled new heights after his appointment.

I knew one female colleague who ran right out of court (and indeed the Bar) in the middle of her submission, such was his rudeness. It was legendary and its excesses were reserved for the prettier females. Of course, in many cases they were the less able to handle him, their experience of life in the law to date teaching them that their prettiness helped to smooth paths rather than roughen them. This left them inadequately equipped to deal with the adversity meted out by Foley. It didn't follow, of course, that Margaret, whose attractiveness was such that Foley might well have to dip into his reserves of rudeness to insult her adequately, would not be able to withstand the onslaught such were her intellectual powers, unlike her pretty peers.

Unfortunately, this subtlety escaped me in the heat of battle and the words were out before I had a chance to assess them. As soon as they were uttered I realised this was a mistake, but it was too late to stop me adding, 'You're not in front of Fleming now.'

'I hope, Dermot, that your forensic skills surpass your diplomatic ones,' she replied. With an expression that suggested she thought me a little pathetic, she marched off. I regretted ever making the remark. The negotiations which were never very promising seemed to have come to an abrupt end.

* * *

Anyway, we were on. Samantha, who by now must have nearly exhausted her supply of chewing gum and who had taken less than a keen interest in the progress of the negotiations, was settling herself in front of me. This consisted of pulling at the loin cloth that passed for a skirt, an admiring glance in her pocket mirror and a rather public application of lipstick.

Beside me, Margaret, with an air of total confidence, spread her papers out on the bench in front of us, not keeping entirely to her own half. A last-minute reference to the documentation, a brief note and a quick word across the bench with her solicitor. There really wasn't much point in me saying anything to Samantha.

'Mr. McNamara, you are for the Plaintiff, I presume?' enquired Judge Foley. 'And who is for the County Council?' knowing perfectly well who, but ventilating his prejudice at an early moment.

'Ms. Thompson, My Lord.'

'I see,' he said resignedly. 'And will this take long, *Miss* Thompson?' his tone suggesting that if it did it would be her fault. I allowed myself a smile. We were getting off on the right note.

'Not unless my friend or Your Lordship lengthens matters, My Lord,' Margaret replies without humour.

Battlelines have been drawn at an early stage and the more Foley and Margaret get stuck into one another, the better from my point of view. However, there is a long way to go.

'There is no need to be disagreeable, Miss Thompson. It is simply that I wish to draw the parties' attention to the fact that I will not be sitting after 3.30.' This announcement is hardly necessary since Foley never sits beyond 3.30. However, it is news to Samantha who cheers up at the prospect of knocking off early.

Anto makes his tieless way to the witness box. '. . . the truth, the whole truth and nothing but the truth'. 'And what is your name?' enquires the Registrar. 'Anto Mullen, Your Worship.' (His Lordship will not like the 'your worship' bit. No matter how much you try to coach them before giving evidence, you can't cover everything.)

'What is your proper name, Mr. Mullen?' enquires the Judge.

'Anto Mullen, Worship.'

'My Lord.'

'No. Anto Mullen, Worship.'

'I mean, you will call me "My Lord", not "Your Worship", Mr. Mullen.'

'I see, Your Lordship,' said Anto, clearly not seeing at all.

'Now, what is your proper name, I mean your full name?'

'Anto Ignatius Mullen, My Worship.'

'My Lord.'

'Sorry, My Lord. Anto Ignatius Mullen.'

'No, no, no, Anto! I mean, Mr. Mullen. What is Anto an abbreviation for?'

'Abbreviation, My Lord?'

'Yes, Mr. Mullen, abbreviation. What is Anto short for?'

'Oh, now I'm with you, Judge. Anhoney, Judge.'

'What?' Foley is barely able to contain himself.

'Anthony,' I help out.

'Oh, I see! Anthony. Thank you, Mr. McNamara. Well, I'll call you Anthony. I mean I'll write down Anthony. I do so detest abbreviations.'

Foley doesn't like abbreviations and he doesn't like Margaret. I suppose the case is evenly matched at the moment.

'Mr. Mullen, you are the Plaintiff in this action?' my opening question.

'The wha?'

'Well, if I put it another way, you are the person bringing this action. Is that right?'

'I suppose so.'

'Well, nobody else is bringing the action, are they, Mr. Mullen?'

'Mr. McNamara!' interrupts Judge Foley, 'I think we can take it that Mr. Mullen is the Plaintiff and that you are acting for him. Now if we could get on to more important matters or there will be no possibility of finishing the case.'

'Of course, My Lord. Now, Mr. Mullen, you live at 25 John Paul Crescent, Belleville?' 'No.' 'You don't?' 'You do,' chorused Mr. Mullen, Senior, and Anto's girlfriend from the well of the Court. 'Well, where do you live then?' enquires the Judge. '25 John Paul Crescent,' shouts up Anto Senior and girlfriend in unison. 'Silence! Mr. McNamara, try and control your witnesses.' 'Yes, My Lord.' 'Well, Mr. Mullen? Do you or do you not live at 25 John Paul Crescent?' 'I suppose I do, My Lord.' 'Well, why did you tell me a moment ago that you did not?' 'Because I spend most of my time at my girlfriend's, which is around the corner.' 'Well, Mr. McNamara, we seem to have solved the mystery as to where your client lives at last. Presumably there are other issues in the case?' 'Of course, My Lord.' (2–1 Margaret.)

As I lead Anto through some more basic background evidence, I am conscious of the problem ahead – that of introducing Judge Foley to Belleville. Foley will certainly not know where Belleville is, may not even have heard of it. The nearest he would have got to Belleville would be flying over it on one of his many show-and-shopping trips to The Mainland. 'How Dublin is expanding,' he is likely to remark over a glass of champagne as he passes over Anto's homeland.

He would be familiar with public parks, of course – Marlay Park, Herbert Park, but not Belleville Park. Places of peace and solitude, walking grounds for young and old, admire the flowers, feed the ducks. Football barely tolerated at a discreet distance. But horses wildly straying, what will he make of that? How will he ever come to terms with Anto's case, namely that he was knocked down by a horse while taking an afternoon stroll in Belleville Park. If he ever saw 'Into the West', he would assume it was a work of fiction.

Inspired by his deep dislike of Margaret, sexual not personal, His Lordship struggles to break down the class barrier that separates himself and Anto.

'I know Marlay Park,' he assists, striking an egalitarian note. 'Would it be anywhere near there?'

'I'm afraid not, My Lord,' I intervene. 'It's on the other side altogether.'

'The other side, Mr. McNamara?'

'The North side, My Lord.'

'Oh.' Judge Foley thought for a moment. 'Portmarnock Golf Club, that's on the North side, I think. I know the golf club well. Anywhere near there?'

'No, My Lord.'

'The airport then. Do I pass it on the way to the airport?'

'Unfortunately not, My Lord. It's nowhere near the airport. Not terrestrially anyway.'

I realise we are getting into deep water. Momentarily, at any rate, the Judge is on our side. Despite himself, he is making valiant efforts to be helpful to Anto. This might not last. Especially if he becomes frustrated over trying to identify where Anto lives. I know there is no landmark within five miles of Belleville and certainly none that would be familiar to His Lordship. I decide to steer him off this line of enquiry.

'I'm afraid that I don't think your Lordship will be familiar with the area at all.'

'Oh, that bad, is it?'

'I have some photographs, My Lord. They will give you an idea of the locus.' I had to interrupt Samantha from her other world. She opened the virgin file that lay in front of her and miraculously the photographs were there, on the very top. His Lordship seemed pleased as I handed up the pictures. Maybe we could put the anonymity of the North side behind us.

But not for long. 'Is this a park?' enquired His Lordship, contrasting in his mind's eye the carpeted lawns of Merrion Square (before they were ceded by the Archbishop, a retrograde step in the Judge's view). Belleville Park appeared as vast tracts of parched and cracked earth, resembling more a building site than a parkland. Not a blade of grass. Not a tulip to be seen. Not a duck. Graffitied walls. Boulders. What would Foley make of all this? Not Foley's idea of a public amenity. Maybe it will provoke his sympathy. Maybe he will take it out on the County Council for forcing people to have to recreate in such conditions. As long as no-one tells him how impossible it is to maintain the area such is the level of vandalism.

Anto doesn't do too badly in the box. The Judge is in benign mood towards him. His antagonism towards Margaret helps him over the cultural and language difficulties that Anto presents. Anto's monosyllabic answers help to keep him within easy reach of the truth. I feel, as I sit down, that His Lordship is well enough disposed towards Anto – an achievement in itself.

I lean towards Samantha. 'How did that go?' 'Dunno. Wasn't listening,' comes the reply, as if taped.

* * *

'Well, Miss Thompson, do you have any questions to ask?' the Judge enquires unnecessarily of Margaret, without as much as looking in her direction.

'One or two, My Lord. Would Your Lordship prefer if I didn't?' retaliates Margaret, not one to take judicial provocation lying down.

'Please ask them then, Miss Thompson. Time is running on, you know.' Margaret rises to her combative feet. I wonder what is in store.

'Anto, you were returning from your walk?' An uncharacteristic error. Margaret, momentarily put out of her stride by the debate with His Lordship and misled by Anto's fresh appearance, forgot that he was of full age and entitled to be so addressed.

Not an opportunity to be missed by His vigilant Lordship. 'Miss Thompson! Please refrain from addressing the witness by his Christian name. We are not in the matrimonial court now. Please be a little more professional.'

Margaret carries on as if the Judge was talking to someone else. 'Mr. Mullen, did you see the horse at all?'

'No, Miss.'

'How very convenient,' Margaret adds.

'I'd ask my friend to refrain from comment, My Lord,' I interject, getting a nervous hand on the bandwagon which was rolling in my favour.

'A very fair objection, Mr. McNamara. Miss Thompson, you can address me at the end of the case if you wish. While cross-examining, you shall confine yourself to question and answer.'

'I know perfectly well how to cross-examine, thank you, My Lord. I'd ask you to ask my learned friend not to interrupt me. I didn't interrupt his examination-in-chief even though peppered with leading questions.'

'Please get on with it, Miss Thompson, if we are not to be here all day.'

'Mr. Mullen, you were walking down towards these houses here?' Margaret asks, resuming her cross-examination. 'Yes, Miss'. 'And where was the wall?' 'Beside the path I was walking on'. 'To your left or right?' 'Left.' 'And your injury, Mr. Mullen? Tell His Lordship which elbow was injured.' 'Right elbow, Miss.' 'How do you explain that, Mr. Mullen?' 'Explain wha', Miss?' 'The fact that the horse pushed you against the wall to your left and you broke your right elbow.' 'Never thought of that, Miss,' he replies in a manner that suggests the inconsistency isn't making much of an impact on him even now. 'Did you not? How very convenient.'

'Comment, My Lord!' I interrupt.

Margaret gives me an impatient glare and continues. 'Have you thought of it now, Mr. Mullen?' 'I have, Miss.' 'And what explanation have you to offer to the Court?'

Unfortunately, the cross-examination has begun to attract His Lordship's attention. 'All I know, Miss, is that is how it happened, exactly as I've told it to you. Not a word of a lie.' Adding after a slight pause, 'Maybe when the horse hit me, it spun me around hitting my right arm against the wall.' Maybe indeed.

'Mr. Mullen, did you ever give a different account of how this accident happened?' 'What do you mean?' 'Did you ever tell anyone that you broke your elbow in a different way?' 'No.' 'For example, when you arrived at the hospital, did you explain to the casualty nurse how the accident happened?' 'No.' 'No? Are you sure?' 'Yes. When I arrived at the hospital I was in shock. I didn't speak to anyone.' 'Did anyone go with you to the hospital?' 'Thomas, I mean Mr. Nolan, came with me in the ambulance.' 'Did he give the nurse an account of your accident?' 'I don't know. I was in shock.' 'Is he in Court?' 'He is.' 'Will he be giving evidence?' 'I don't know.' 'Finally, Mr. Mullen, I suggest that you are lying when you say the horse knocked you down.'

'Miss Thompson!' interrupts His Lordship, 'This is a personal injury case. People don't lie in personal injury cases. They may be mistaken in their recollection, but lying is too strong.'

'My Lord, not to put a tooth in it, the Defendant's case is that the Plaintiff is lying and that he was never knocked down by a horse. It's a fraudulent claim, My Lord, and you will be so satisfied at the end of the evidence, but if Your Lordship insists I will rephrase the question. Mr. Mullen, I put it to you that you are mistaken when you say that the horse pushed you against the wall?'

'You may think I'm lying, Miss, but I'm not. As sure as God's my witness, I'm not lying. I'm on oath here and what I'm telling you, Your Worship, is the truth.'

'Mr. Mullen, I put it to you that you were not struck by the horse. Rather, you were on the horse. Mr. Mullen, were you riding the horse at the time when you fell off?'

'No, Miss. I can't ride. And anyway I'm afraid of horses.'

'Thank you, Mr. Mullen.'

Margaret sat down. Pleased with herself. Not triumphant. Not yet. Just pleased. Her expression suggested triumph-postponed. She had me worried.

So had Foley. Despite his antipathy towards her, Margaret had hauled him back. She had left him with a few questions to chew over, along with his pencil. He was looking back over his notes. Frankly, in the lateness of the consultation, I had missed the fact that the wall was on the left and the fracture on the right. That in itself took some explaining.

But the real problem was the casualty nurse. Clearly, Margaret had the hospital notes and someone had given a different account of Anto's accident to the nurse. What was that account and how damaging would it be? I recalled our negotiations and how Margaret kept hinting at things which she couldn't or wouldn't fully share, but which would become clear later. I concluded that the chances were that this evidence would be very damaging indeed.

This development presented me with a decision which would have to be made immediately. Whether or not to call Thomas Nolan. Margaret may be bluffing and she may not have the casualty nurse in Court, in which case she could not adduce this evidence about the accident unless Thomas admitted that he had told the nurse how the accident occurred. Apart from other more aesthetic reasons, this would be a sound legal reason for not calling Mr. Nolan. On the other hand, if Margaret wasn't bluffing and she had the nurse in Court or available (I looked around the Courtroom quickly and couldn't spot anyone who fitted the job description), the nurse's evidence of what Mr. Nolan said to her about the accident, uncontradicted by Mr. Nolan himself, would more than likely be fatal.

In any event, without Mr. Nolan to give his grandstand evidence of the assault by the horse, Judge Foley would be left with an unexplained accident and no possibility at all of pinning the County Council with liability. My mind was almost made up. I leaned across the table.

'Samantha, what do you think? Should we call Nolan or not?'

'You haven't any choice, have you?' replied Samantha, to my astonishment.

'Thank you, Samantha,' I said to myself.

* * *

'Mr. McNamara, is that your case?' His Lordship enquired, a trifle impatiently. I must have been taking a little longer than I thought to resolve my legal difficulties.

'One more witness, My Lord. Come up please, Mr. Nolan'. Mr. Nolan, who had the unfortunate disadvantage of looking like someone who may never have told the truth in his life, made his less than straight way to the witness box.

Were it not for the presence of Margaret, Judge Foley's patience with the unemployed classes in general and with Anto in particular would be long since exhausted and Anto would be well on his way back to his life of impecuniosity with an, albeit academic, order for costs against him to boot. But Margaret was keeping us in there with a chance. Not for any incompetence on her part, far from it, but because His Lordship was more prejudiced against women than the working and unworking classes. If he was at home with unworking classes, they did not come from Belleville or its environs. For how much longer could this Battle of the Prejudices continue in our favour?

To be fair to Anto, he had done as well as could be expected. Caused to pause in his tracks somewhat in the course of cross-examination maybe, but still in the saddle, as it were. But what about Thomas?

Thomas worried me. We still had a long way to go and a lot of hurdles to clear. But Thomas could bring us down all too abruptly. First of all, he liked to talk. If Anto bordered on the inarticulate, it was not a territory familiar to Thomas. He was difficult to stop and, of course, the more he would say, the more difficult it was to keep him to a version which, if not quite the truth, might at least be plausible. He would say whatever he thought might help Anto's case. When I pointed out some discrepancy in his evidence to him at the consultation, his response was to enquire, 'What do you want me to say?' Never a very auspicious enquiry from a witness. In addition, he fancied himself as a bit of a wit. I told him to leave the jokes to the Judge and to answer 'Yes' and 'No' where at all possible. It was like telling the Pope to introduce women priests forthwith. A sort of glazed expression crossed his face.

I guided Thomas as best I could through his evidence, leading him as much as possible. Margaret was silent throughout, which was unusual for her. Then she started.

'Mr. Nolan, are you normally in your bedroom at 3.30 on a winter's afternoon?'

'Only if I'm tired, Miss,' replied Thomas, trying to be funny.

'What were you doing there on this afternoon, Mr. Nolan?'

'What do you normally do in your bedroom, Miss?'

'There's no need to be smart and I'll ask the questions, you answer them. Well, what were you doing?'

'Do I have to answer that question, Judge?'

'The witness is right, Miss Thompson. Of what possible relevance could it be to this case to know what this witness was doing in his bedroom at 3.30 on this wet afternoon? What is relevant is what happened to Mr. Mullen in the park, not what happened to Mr. Nolan in his bedroom in the afternoon, Miss Thompson. So what if he was playing with his model railway?'

'Your Lordship is most helpful,' bristled Margaret. 'I would be grateful if Your Lordship would allow me to continue my cross-examination without being interrupted. I have only just begun and your Lordship is in protecting the witness. Will your Lordship permit the question?'

'Very well, Miss Thompson. *De bene esse.*'

'Day wha', Judge?'

'Never mind, Nolan, just answer the question.'

'What was the question?' (Well done, Margaret.)

'Mr. Nolan, I was asking you what you were doing in your bedroom at 3.30 on this December afternoon. Would you mind telling the Court?'

'I would mind.'

'Well, Mr. Nolan, I'm afraid the Judge has ruled that you have to answer the question.'

Thomas' voice dropped. 'Em.' Pause.

'Yes, Mr. Nolan?'

Hesitantly, 'I had the house to myself for the afternoon and I had invited the girlfriend over. Well, you know yourself, Miss. We had just gone up to the bedroom for a bit of . . .'

'Mr. Nolan!' protested Ms. Thompson, realising a little too late that this line of questioning had already gone too far.

'Miss Thompson!' protested the Judge. I sat silent.

'My Lord?' pleaded Ms. Thompson, vulnerable for the first time in the case and perhaps in her career.

'Miss Thompson, I warned against the question on the basis of relevance, but you insisted and now you have got your answer. Perhaps for the rest of the case you would confine yourself to the issues and not go off on exploratory tangents.'

'Yes, My Lord,' replied Margaret, temporarily and uncharacteristically chastened.

I was humming to myself. Samantha too, but that had nothing to do with the development of the case. Even the Judge seemed pleased. Come back from that, Margaret.

Margaret was anxious to get out of the bedroom as quickly as she could, but she had to delay a little longer. 'You accept, Mr. Nolan, that it was misty and that visibility was not very good?'

'I do.'

'You heard me ask Mr. Mullen how he explained breaking his right elbow when he was walking towards your house and the wall was on his left. How do you explain it, Mr. Nolan?'

'Anto, I mean Mr. Mullen, was not walking in that direction at all. He was walking in the opposite direction, away from me. I only saw his back.' (Brilliant, Thomas. I mean, Mr. Nolan. Brilliant thinking on your feet. Should think of becoming a barrister.)

'But, Mr. Nolan, your friend says he was walking towards you.' Margaret wasn't going to let him away with that.

'Well, he wasn't. He was concussed, remember, and that might explain why he is confused as to the direction in which he was walking.'

'And, Mr. Nolan, you yourself said a few moments ago in reply to Mr. McNamara that he was walking towards you.'

'Did I? Are you sure?' Foley goes back over his notes, but can't find anything. 'If I did, then it was a mistake. I meant to say he was walking away from me. Because he was. I remember it well.'

'What about the horse, Mr. Nolan? Surely the Plaintiff would have seen the horse coming towards him?' interposed the Judge, who was manifestly wide awake.

The question stymied Thomas for a moment or two and then he answered, 'The horse had been running in my direction, but then did a U-turn and ran towards Mr. Mullen and threw him against the wall.'

'And your friend didn't see any of this happening?'

'Apparently not, Judge, but that's how it happened. Maybe he was affected by the mist.'

Not very convincing. But the Judge decided to leave it at that. I had a sneaking suspicion that the balance of prejudices was shifting slightly and away from Anto. Margaret had regained her composure and, with it, control.

★ ★ ★

As she regained His Lordship's interest, Margaret judged it opportune to leave the bedroom behind and head for the hospital. 'Mr. Nolan, we know you travelled in the ambulance with your friend and we know that he was at first concussed and then in shock and didn't have any conversation with the casualty nurse. Therefore it must have been you who spoke to her. Is that correct?'

'Was she a blondy one?' 'It doesn't really matter what colour she was. Did you or did you not have a conversation with her?' 'It's so long ago, Miss, I don't really remember. I suppose I may have.' 'Does that mean you did?' 'I suppose it does.' 'Did you tell her how your friend met with this accident?' 'I may have, I can't remember.' 'Did you tell her your friend fell off a horse?' 'Can you repeat the question?' 'I think you heard the question, Mr. Nolan. Did you tell the casualty nurse that your friend fell off a horse?' 'No. I don't think so. I'd never have said something like that.' 'Why not?' 'Because he didn't fall off a horse.' 'Tell His Lordship what you did say about the accident to the casualty nurse.'

Thomas paused and paled. He thought for a moment, trying to recall what he said to the nurse. Margaret allowed him the silence. The Judge looked up from his note-taking. Even Samantha turned around. The dénouement. This better be good, Thomas.

'I told her that Anto had had a falling out with a horse.' (Brilliant, I thought to myself.) A titter went around the Courtroom at this piece of ingenuity. Margaret didn't get a chance to dig in. His Lordship was there before her.

'Mr. Nolan, do you expect me to believe that what you said to the nurse was that your friend had a falling out with a horse? Not that he fell off the horse?'

'That's it, Judge. That's what I told her. It is as clear to me now as if it were yesterday.'

'And what's more that the horse, which at one moment was heading towards your bedroom, suddenly did a U-turn and doubled back and collided with Mr. Mullen?'

'You have it in one, Judge. The barrister said you were very clever.'

'Any more questions, *Ms.* Thompson?'

'No, My Lord,' replied Margaret, reading the signs and resuming her seat in deferred triumph.

'Is that your evidence, Mr. McNamara?'

'Yes, My Lord.'

'Do you have an application to make, Ms. Thompson?'

'I do, My Lord.'

'Granted. Case dismissed.'

'But, My Lord, Your Lordship hasn't heard me as to why there shouldn't be a direction in the case and why the County Council should be made go into evidence.'

'Very well, Mr. McNamara. What do you have to say?'

I addressed him as hopelessly as I did briefly. His mind was made up. He indulged me a little longer than he wanted to.

'Thank you, Mr. McNamara. I have heard all your evidence. I have listened to your submissions. There isn't a doubt in my mind as to where the truth lies in this case. I have given the Plaintiff every chance to make his case and establish his credibility. (And to be fair to old Foley, for once he had.)

'Mr. Mullen asks me to believe that as he was walking towards Mr. Nolan's house, he was pushed against a wall to his left, thereby breaking his right arm. Ms. Thompson correctly draws attention to the unlikelihood of this. Mr. Nolan, who apparently is not a friend though they live near one another and are of an age, knows better what Mr. Mullen was doing than Mr. Mullen himself. Apparently Mr. Mullen was walking in the opposite direction to that in which he says he was walking and the runaway horse did a U-turn and collided with him. And this explains the fracture to the right arm. And then we have the conversation with the casualty nurse. A falling out with a horse indeed. Do Messrs. Mullen and Nolan think that I live in an ivory tower? I started off this case with a certain sympathy for the Plaintiff which step by step has been eroded by Ms. Thompson's unravelling of the Plaintiff's evidence. I have no doubt but that the Plaintiff and his non-friend are lying to me. Ms. Thompson is quite right, this is a fraudulent claim and I am very tempted to send the papers to the DPP. Dismiss the claim.'

'Costs, My Lord?'

'Costs, Ms. Thompson.'

I had never seen Foley so worked up. He bolted from the Bench. Margaret gathered her papers together and without as much as a glance in my direction exited elegantly from the arena. By the time Samantha and I reached the endless corridor, the Belleville jockeys were gone.

I decided that there had to be some consolation and invited Samantha for a coffee, but apparently there was some urgent work to be done in the office.

As I made my way down the corridor and back towards the Library, I wondered what my wife would say about another (what she called VdeP) Brief from Arnold, who could, of course, boast about the social service he so selflessly provides.

★ ★ ★

7

Bahamas (1973) Limited v. McGinley

(Unreported, Circuit Court, 2 February 1993)

One of the hallmarks of civilization in Ireland at the close of the 20th century is the accessibility of all its parts. Or so I thought.

'Return ticket, please. First class to Letterkenny,' I bellowed. It wasn't a question of 'money no object'. I had given the matter a lot of thought and decided to splash out on a first-class ticket so I could do some work on the journey.

'I'm afraid there isn't one,' came the reply.

'What? No first class?'

'No, sir. No train. I am afraid there is no train service to Letterkenny,' replied a slightly surprised Iarnród Éireann official.

I was completely taken aback. I was sure there was a train to Letterkenny. What is more, Ronald had as much as told me there was one. Hadn't he given me the time of departure – 5.30, Sunday evening?

Ronald Browning and I had been in College together, though never very closely together. When we came to the Bar, I remained in Dublin whereas he went on the North Western Circuit, where, by all accounts, most notably his own, he was doing very nicely thank you. We were never bosom buddies. He thought me a little stuffy. I thought him a little silly.

I was aware of the reputation certain Circuits had for their unwelcoming attitude to itinerant barristers. I knew some colleagues who had been metamorphosed into stalactites (or is it stalagmites?) such was the frostiness of their reception, not to mention others who were rendered mute for the want of someone to talk to. Such thoughts crossed my mind for a brief moment as I struggled for an explanation as to why there was no train to Letterkenny or, more precisely, why I had been led to believe that there might be. Was I so unwelcome on the Circuit? Such a potential threat? So feared as an opponent the following morning? In my flight of paranoia, I was losing touch with reality. A simple misunderstanding, surely?

I thought I would give it another go. Perhaps the rail official had a hangover or thought I had said 'Letterfrack'. Perhaps it was his first day and he didn't yet know where his trains went.

'Are you sure?' I enquired to his astonishment.

He looked at me in much the same way that he might have had I asked him if he was sure his name was not Julio Iglesias. For a moment, I thought he might ask me for proof that I were not totally insane. He compromised.

'Quite sure. The last train to Letterkenny was in 1960. Great Northern Railways. I should know. I drove it.'

I was beginning to panic. It was now 5.15 on Sunday evening. Come hell or high water, I had to be in the Courthouse in Letterkenny at 9.25 the next morning. I turned pleadingly to Rachel beside me. Could I have the car? Our car? Her car? Apparently not. As she had already explained to me, she needed it for an important consultation uptown tomorrow. Of course.

The car (a convertible Golf) was an occasional source of frisson between us in an otherwise frisson-free relationship. As far as I was concerned anyway. Any other married couple we knew of our vintage, or even younger, whether in or out of the Library, had the advantage of two cars. We only had the one and even that we came late to. We had worked out a general understanding in relation to its use, however. Rachel used it. Quite simple, really. After all, her father had bought it for her. I always felt that my equity in it was, to say the least, underrated.

Rachel did not rely exclusively on the fact that her father had bought the car to justify her monopoly. After all, my father had paid our rent for the first few years, but that didn't stop Rachel sharing the flat. No. As she persuasively pointed out, my professional route was from flat to Library and home again, and there was a perfectly adequate bus and DART service available to meet my transportation needs. Her needs were different, of course. She would have to stop off for consultations in both directions. Hence, the car was to her indispensable. In addition, we had a policy of not driving in and out together. Indeed, we didn't even socialise together once in the Library.

I wouldn't have minded all that much, but Rachel said that it was not a good idea.

By now, therefore, I had become accustomed to public transport and, upon enquiry, passed off necessity as a preference. However, I had changed allegiance from bus to DART.

* * *

For a while now, we have lived in a wave-swept basement flat in Seapoint. Our terrace looks across Dublin Bay towards Howth. The house beside us, the entire of it naturally, is owned by a captain of industry and his wife. A mutual friend predicted that no sooner would we be in the door than our neighbour would be popping the bubbly. True to the prophecy, the furniture removers had barely removed themselves when there was a knock on the door and an invitation to a champagne reception.

From the word go, we got on like a house on fire. The following Monday, I was waiting for a bus outside Goggins when, with a great bipping of horn, this magnificent convertible Jaguar paused a little beyond my bus-stop. Unaware that I knew anyone of such class and failing to recognize my champagne host from the weekend, I ignored the fanfare. But not for long. More bipping and frantic waving and eventually I identified my industrial captain from next door. As I hurdled the half-door, he wanted to know what I was doing hanging around Goggins at that hour of the morning. Did I not know that it wouldn't be open for some hours yet? I don't think he heard my explanation, that I was waiting for a bus, as we slipped through the gears to the accompaniment of 'Brave New World'. There and then I decided to travel by DART, a more suitable statement, I thought, for one who lives beside a captain of industry.

Anyway, back to Amiens Street (as I insist on knowing it) and my immediate transportation difficulty. No train. Apparently no car either. How was I going to get to Letterkenny? One last unavailing appeal to the intransigent Rachel. What had started off as a matter of cosmetics had become a matter of logistics. It might have been nice to have had the car in Letterkenny. Arrive in style. A touch of class. Independence. Would you like a lift to the restaurant, Arnold? Mr. Wilkinson? Strike the right note. Success breeds success. This was no longer the issue. Whether or not I would be in Letterkenny at all to do the case, discharge my duty to my client, impress Mr. Wilkinson with my forensic skills, was what was now at stake. Suddenly, Rachel's insistence on her upmarket consultation the following day was looking a small bit unreasonable.

'What about a bus?' suggested the official, rushing to what should have been Rachel's embarrassment.

'What about a bus?' I asked back. 'Oh. You mean, get a bus to Letterkenny?'

'Precisely. Busáras is just across the road.'

There being no sign of the convertible Jag and less sign of a climb-down by Rachel, there was little else for it but to scurry across the road with my Samsonite suitcase (a present from my mother on my call to the Bar), with Rachel following in our car. As if to make up for the fact that there was no train, any number of buses were leaving Busáras for Letterkenny at 5.30. I only needed one of them. Good value too, at £13 return. Or so it seemed.

I went to a lot of trouble to get a seat beside the window and nearly as much trouble to wave in the direction of Rachel's back as she accelerated out of the bus station.

Apparently, arrival time was 9.30. So, four hours to cover half of Ireland. You could be halfway to Cape Town. Or Calcutta. I vowed to make good use of the time and to get some paperwork done, even without the train and without the first class, and if I did that, then I would treat myself to the nearest hotel to the Courthouse instead of a B&B.

In the haste of my calculations, I had forgotten that, since it was February, it would be dark before we reached Finglas and so to read I would need an overhead light. No-one had told me an overhead light was an optional extra. Though I doubt if it was ever part of Bus Éireann's plan that anyone should read by them. So much for my good intentions and the road to hell. Not to mention Letterkenny and a nice hotel room. 'The best laid plans of mice and men' . . . Nice one, Robbie, you understood life alright.

This case was not exactly getting off on the right note. Nothing for it but to settle into my seat and the falling night.

We were not far out of the City when I began to wonder if I

hadn't boarded a Valentine Night's Express. Everyone around me seemed to be romantically linked in one physical form or another. The girl beside me was heavily engaged in that well-known Oriental love game 'Chinese Nosing' with the young man in front of her who, better than any Olympic gymnast, was able so to contort his body and his seat that for all practical purposes he was facing his partner, even though all seats were forward facing. I felt a complete gooseberry and knew that it was only a matter of time until one of them plucked up the courage to ask me to swap seats. This thought sealed my determination to hold onto my window seat. To this end, I folded up my lanky body as best I could, tilting it towards the passing countryside, and began to stare out into the gloom as if I had some remarkable interest therein. Anything to avoid the eye contact which would inevitably form the basis of a request to exchange accommodation.

The frenzied activity was less easy to avoid. He was running his hands up and down her uncovered legs in a most provocative fashion. It was certainly provoking me. How must it have been provoking them? If it didn't stop soon, and we were only at the beginning of the journey, it wouldn't be my seat he would be looking for. Riven with envy, I thought to ask him to desist from his forays up and down her shapely limbs. As quickly, I realised that this would probably have no effect and that a complaint to the driver would probably be equally ineffectual. Even worse, lover-boy would likely take advantage of my momentary absence to take over my seat.

Then I thought that, since there were already so many hands travelling up and down her thighs, she might not notice another one or two, and in this way a certain parity of enjoyment could be achieved. The unspoken differences that had arisen between us could be resolved and we could get on with the business of getting to Letterkenny in comfort and harmony. On that warm note, I began to doze but not before, for safety sake, I had tied both my hands to the leg – of my seat.

My repose did not last long. My head so bumped off the window that I was worried about brain damage. It was impossible to get a comfortable position. When I awoke from whatever you might call what I had fallen into, I was decidedly uncomfortable. My legs ached for lack of space. Elsewhere ached for reasons best known to my neighbouring lovers. A queasy feeling was overwhelming my stomach, which was not helped by Cleopatra's graphic account of vomiting all over the kitchen table. I missed the build-up to this punchline, so I cannot share with you why she felt this biographical gem was worth incorporating into her pillow talk. I may well have a friend whose proudest boast is that his beautiful wife does everything with elegance including vomiting and while I readily admit succumbing to the attractions of Cleopatra's legs, I seriously doubted if her encounter with the kitchen table ranked among her most elegant moments. Suffice to say that the anecdote did nothing to reassure my stomach.

I looked with even more intent at the passing darkness. Is there anything more depressing that the Irish Midlands on a wet Sunday night in February? As spied through the steamy window of a Bus Éireann coach? Field upon flooding field, town upon drizzling town, village upon deserted village and, if not deserted, why not, for God's sake. Chinese take-away, video store, Wel-Cum Inn. Onward and onward. Relentless heave and roll of the Bus Éireann coach bearing you on. Over a road that more closely resembled a pock-marked jumping arena than any EU-funded motorway. You took it on trust that you were being carried closer to your destination.

The highlight of the excursion was a brief stop in Monaghan for refreshment or toilet. One or other. Certainly not both. There isn't time. Or there would be if there weren't queues due to the fact that the bus schedules are arranged in such a way that as many buses as possible pull up at the same time. The purpose of the stop is two-fold – to see how many passengers get no refreshment at all and to see how many passengers get left behind or, if things really go according to plan, how many board wrong buses and speed off in alternative directions.

My night was up there with the best of them. Few got refreshments. Fewer consumed them. Three got left behind. And three sped off in alternative directions.

Just as I sat down in the depot with my modest food parcel I saw a bus, my bus I thought, make a forward movement. I deemed it prudent to abandon my purchase and go in pursuit. I was lucky to spot my mistake in time to board the correct bus. As we left the depot, I heard the announcement of the departure of the last bus that night to Letterkenny – a fraction of a second too late for anyone who had not reacted with my earlier prescience to do anything about it. Bus Éireann 3 : Passengers 0.

* * *

As we accelerated towards the Border, I turned my mind to the purpose of my journey. If it wasn't clear already, then I can now confirm that this case represented a new departure for me in terms of my practice. For a start, I rarely went out on Circuit. But, more importantly, this was not a personal injury case. To date this was the only type of case I had done for Arnold or indeed anyone else (though there were not many others). Don't get me wrong. I am not knocking running-down cases. Most of us depend on them for our livelihood. It is just that surely I am not going to spend the rest of my career at the Bar asking witnesses if they blew their horn or saw the yoghurt on the floor of the supermarket or if they had more good days than bad or were they recovered from the whiplash injury that no-one had heard of twenty years ago.

Surely, there was more to a career at the Bar than that? More to a life? What about the great issues of our time? The right to life? To death? A gay marriage? Should a woman be allowed to be impregnated with the sperm of her deceased husband?

My present case fell a little short of those dizzy heights, but was a small step in the right direction nonetheless. A case in contract. No great ethical issue. No need to peruse the Constitution. Unlikely to make even the local newspapers. But progress nonetheless. Away for a day from what a broken leg is worth and towards Law, beautiful Law.

After all, what were all those years at the King's Inns for? All those subjects with such lofty titles. Jurisprudence, Private International Law, the Law of Real Property, the Law of Intellectual Property and the Holy Spirit of the Law, Equity. Not a sign anywhere of the Law of Personal Injury and yet it is the only law I have had sight of since coming into the Library.

In truth, my present case was little more than debt-collection. But there was a sniff of sophistication about some of the issues raised by the defence, such as implied terms, repudiation, fundamental breach. I may have to cite a case or two, quote from a learned

Judgment, make legal submissions. Glory beckoned.

There was nothing unusual about Arnold calling me in the Library at 4.00 on a Friday afternoon with a Brief for the following Monday. Nothing unusual at all. In fact, on this Friday afternoon I had decided to pull up stumps earlier than usual so that he was lucky to get me, though he might not have quite seen it like that. On the other hand, come 4.00 o'clock and your first choices are unavailable, you are lucky to get anyone, particularly if it is to travel to Letterkenny.

I had just finished a review-of-the-week cup of coffee with Matthew. There is always quite a buzz in the coffee room on a Friday afternoon. The highs and lows of the week have settled down. Colleagues are more relaxed. The weekend stretches itself before one like an annual vacation. So much time. All the things that one will get done; all not done by Monday morning, but that depression seems light years away.

Matthew had had a busier week than I, or so he said. Indeed, so he usually said. He may have been right. I hadn't been very busy since Christmas. The Term, this one a long one, hadn't yet got off the ground as far as I was concerned. But there was still time. Unfortunately, when he enquired, my diary was blank for the week ahead also. There was a Motion entered for the Wednesday, but my solicitor had phoned me earlier in the day to say that it was to be adjourned for a month. No money (or, for that matter, boasting) in adjournments.

Not surprisingly, seeing that he enquired about my diary, Matthew's diary was quite busy for the following week. Quite busy to him. Jam-packed to me. I gave a not-so-veiled hint that if he needed any assistance . . . I was beginning to think that this cup of coffee had not been a good idea. Not good for morale. Undermining of the feel-good factor, so important at the commencement of the weekend. Mental note not to have coffee with Matthew again and certainly not on Friday afternoons.

If only Arnold had called me half an hour earlier, I would have been able to say to Matthew that I was off to Letterkenny on Monday. That would surely have impressed him. Look a bit odd, I thought, if I dropped over to his desk now and announced casually, 'By the way, Matthew, going to Letterkenny on Monday. Completely slipped my mind when I was talking to you. See you Tuesday.'

It was part of Arnold's modus operandi to leave things to the last moment. Forward planning was not one of his strengths. Inefficiency accounted for the fact that he was looking for a barrister for Monday on Friday afternoon. The fact that it was so late on Friday afternoon when I was called out simply reflects my place in his honours list. In the early stages of our professional relationship, I had innocently assumed that it was me and no-one else that Arnold wanted for the particular case. In time, I was disabused of this piece of self-flattery by the sheer number of colleagues who had asked me if I had been able to help Arnold out. Indispensability, how are you? The Brief you thought your very own turns out to have been all over the place. A tart of a Brief.

Coffee with Matthew had left me a little depressed. Five to four: unlikely that anything was going to turn up at that stage. Thought I'd slope off to an early weekend. Normally I would go the whole way and hang around till 5.00. Partly in case anything might materialise, partly to pick up the tail-of-the-week gossip. Around that time, the Library sheds its professional mask, powders its nose and dons a more light-hearted pose. The weekend begins. Some of the girls who have slipped off earlier in the afternoon for a shower and a change reappear. The fellows too. The fraudulent preference and oppression of minorities that so preoccupied them a short hour ago have vanished to be replaced by 'Where will we start? Downstairs? Sky Bar? Hughes?' Happily, all that was behind me. I had had my innings. Short perhaps, but I had been there.

I was tidying my desk. Nothing to take home. Thought I would wander up the quays, slip into Virgin to buy a CD, pick up two take-aways in Monkstown and a video ('Four Weddings and a Funeral' maybe, I wanted to see it again) and have a cosy evening with Rachel beside the waves. That is, if Rachel was in. Some Friday nights, particularly if she had had a busy week, she liked to go out and unwind with some of her colleagues.

* * *

'Dermot McNamara' – a voice from nowhere boomed.

Now who could that be at this hour in the week? I was just changing the message on my answering machine. More than likely a colleague looking for me to go for a drink. The bewitching hour. Many a weekend's plan had been turned on its head by going for a drink at this hour ('Just one, mind. To beat the traffic.'). I made my way through the emptying Library to the door.

It was Arnold. 'How are you fixed for Monday, Dermot?'

That fateful question. No matter how often I am asked it, I cannot come up with a satisfactory formula in reply. If I answer 'Fine', who knows what I am letting myself in for? If I say 'Tied up', perhaps I am turning down a good Brief. Snookered again. No assistance from Arnold. At 4.00 on a Friday afternoon, he cannot afford another refusal. He wants a positive reply. Then he will give me all the information I need. Not before. He is not going to add something that will tempt me to turn it down. Not that I am likely to do that anyway. (Go for it, Dermot. Positive waves.)

'Free as a bird actually, Arnold.'

Surprise, surprise. I suppose I should spin him some yarn about something else having settled or that I must consult my diary, but I am not in the mood.

'Contract case. (Contract. Now that is a surprise. But why me?) Letterkenny.' (Ah. That explains it. And if it didn't, Arnold went on to. Not putting a tooth in it.)

'Dermot, I think you should know that this is an important case. (The idea of Arnold handling anything important . . .) Mr. Wilkinson is taking a personal interest in it and will be travelling with us. It is something of a test case and they'll (whoever they are) be watching it back at HQ. We would like you to do your best. (Did they think I might throw the case?)

'In fairness,' he continued, 'you should know that I had hoped Peter or Michael would be free, but they are engaged in the Motion List here on Monday. (Likely, but unlikely, if you know what I mean. The simple fact is that the case is in Letterkenny. Nobody goes to Letterkenny except the holy souls who have to. And me, of course. Even if you ask me at 4.00 on a Friday afternoon. My time to be choosey will come, later rather than sooner, it would appear.)

'I called them out and each of them suggested you. (How cosy. What you might call a well-disguised hatchet job.)

'In fact, Mr. Wilkinson suggested young Ronald Browning. Apparently he is making a bit of a name for himself and Mr. W felt that as we were coming from outside, it might be a good idea to brief someone on the Circuit. Anyway, Ronald is on the other side, so he can't do it either.' (Salt in the wound. Hardly anyone left in the Library really.)

Arnold handed me the papers, a more presentable bundle than usual. 'Mr. Wilkinson and I are going to travel up early on Sunday. Stay in the "Slieve Russell" and have a round of golf there and drive on to Letterkenny on Monday morning. What about a consultation? I suppose 9.25? See you at the Courthouse. Enjoy your weekend.'

It's always the same. Not a word of thanks. No apology for briefing you at such short notice. Quite the opposite. 'Couldn't get anyone else, do read the Brief, do win the case and aren't you lucky.' Once again, how accurate Robbie's words: 'The best laid plans . . .' How well he knew human nature. Pity he never wrote in English. I must remember to have them typed up and pin them over my desk.

New message on the answering machine. Cancel CD and video. No need to cancel Rachel as she didn't show anyway until the early hours; apparently it had been a particularly busy week and there was a lot of unwinding to do.

* * *

I spent Friday night perusing *Bahamas (1973) Limited v. McGinley*, the facts of which were a little exotic. I reviewed them now as we endured the dark delights of the 'North West Passage' as the tail-end of our odyssey to Letterkenny is endearingly called by Bord Fáilte.

If the case were ever to be reported in the 'Irish Reports' (now there's a fantasy for a dark wet night), the headnote would probably run something like this: 'Bahamas (1973) Limited – a company registered in Panama – buys and sells coconuts – one of the world's largest coconut companies – appoints Joseph McGinley (Defendant) sole agent in Ireland – Defendant's first agency – Plaintiff sells £20,000 worth of coconuts to Defendant – coconuts diseased – defective goods – implied term – fundamental breach – Defendant refuses to pay – Plaintiff claims – Circuit Court – Defendant says not liable – counterclaim for £5,000 for losses arising out of agency.'

The particular disease contracted by the coconuts was an especially virulent ailment peculiar to coconuts. Unfortunately, it does not manifest itself outwardly for some considerable time and in the early stages no amount of external examination will reveal the condition. The chances are that the coconut will be well into the home of the ultimate consumer before it becomes apparent that all is not well. At that stage, the intending consumer returns the coconut to his or her greengrocer where a refund is demanded.

Sometimes the consumer gets around to actually fulfilling the coconut's destiny – namely, consuming it – with the result that he or she and the entire of the family fall prey to a particularly foul dose of gastroenteritis. This latter situation invariably leads to the greengrocer's next bundle of post including a Writ for damages.

Whichever the situation, the consumer is unhappy and, at the very least, insists on a refund. This leads to an even more unhappy greengrocer and when the 'Association of Less-than-ecstatic Greengrocers in Ireland' refuses to pay Mr. McGinley, Sole Agent, the latter is left with no alternative but to withhold payment from Bahamas (1973) Limited.

It is a straightforward claim therefore, for the price of goods, coconuts, sold and delivered. With an equally straightforward defence, or so it would appear at first unknowledgeable sight. It doesn't seem unreasonable to contend that McGinley shouldn't have to pay for bad coconuts.

However, that would be to leave one vital piece of the jigsaw out of the legal equation. Up and down the coconut world, from the time when milk was first sucked from its hairy breast, the coconut market was conducted on the premise that the buyer takes the risk. No matter how flawed, no matter how diseased, from the moment when the bargain is struck, the buyer owes the price. This is what in law is known as an 'implied term of the contract' and it is on this implied term that my confidence in the case is founded.

The austerity of this provision has been considerably tempered in recent times by the availability of insurance. Such insurance is cheap and as axiomatic as holiday insurance. It is as inconceivable that a sole agent, such as McGinley, would be unaware of the availability of insurance as that he would be unaware that the buyer carries the coconut, as it were.

But in this case, two in one. McGinley claimed that he did not know that he would have to pay for worthless coconuts. After all, he had been in other markets and there was no such rule. In addition, he had not taken out insurance. This outing to Letterkenny would never have taken place had Mr. McGinley done what was done without complaint and with promptitude by every other coconut sole agent around the world, namely, paid the modest insurance premium.

As for Mr. Wilkinson, his involvement was by way of subrogation (a word I was never comfortable with until I looked it up in my rice-paper Halsbury late on Friday night). 'Subrogation', it reads, 'meaning the substitution of one person or thing for another, so that the same rights and duties which attached to the original person or thing attached to the substituted one, e.g. an insurer is subrogated to the rights of the insured on paying his claim.' Exactly what I thought.

Bahamas had insured the contract with Mr. W's company under an import credit insurance scheme, so that when the company paid Bahamas its losses, the company was then entitled to sue McGinley in the name of Bahamas. Hence, Mr. Wilkinson's presence.

Earlier in my career at the Bar, I would have described this as an open-and-shut case. However, experience had chastened me. There was no such case. In fact, that was the very one to watch. Notwithstanding, and while giving complacency a wide berth, I could not avoid the conclusion that this was a case I was likely to win.

* * *

I was roused gently from my homework by the voice of my driver awarding judgment and costs to the Bahamas and announcing our imminent arrival in Letterkenny.

It was late and dark and wet in Letterkenny and not much fun dragging my mother's present from B&B to B&B. As luck would have it, there was a Jehovah's Witness Conference in town that weekend, so the guesthouses were full, although I suspect that while I might have qualified for the Bus Éireann Best Dressed Traveller Award at the commencement of the journey, by now, in the shabbiness of my soaking suit, the B&B proprietors might well have had second thoughts about me, even if their rooms had been as empty as the Letterkenny streets.

Not a room to be had. Nothing for it, but to abandon the search for budget accommodation and off to the Courtside Hotel and its attendant delights. A hot bath, room service, trousers into trouser press, phone Rachel and a good night's sleep.

Well, three out of five wasn't bad. No answer from Rachel and the witnesses to Jehovah were giving witness to matters more mundane as they raved the night away at their end-of-conference disco. Location? Immediately below my room. For this reason, the good night's sleep did not begin until after 2.00am.

I was in plenty of time for my 9.25 consultation. Entering an unfamiliar Courthouse is a little daunting. As you stride through the grandiose portal (that is what barristers do, are born and groomed to do, to stride through no mere entrance, but a portal) with your black brief bag (hallmark of the Circuit-going barrister) on your back, ambivalence slows the stride. After all, once in, you can go either left or right or even straight ahead. But which? And so many people looking. And so important to get it right. You are in the legal domain now and you must know what you are doing, you must be in control. Even in the small things, like getting to the Bar Room.

In Dundalk, there is even a fourth option. Up. You can ascend the steep flight of stairs that rise in front of you. As I did on my last visit, in all my confidence, because on my previous attendance that is where the Bar Room had been. But no longer was – renovations – no-one told me. Until, at the top, I popped my head into the used-to-be Robing Room, now taken over by a bevy of busy typing ladies and a few token gentlemen a little taken aback by the appearance of this already disrobing barrister. On the long descent, I wondered on what step Morcambe (or would it be Wise?) would put his arm around me, singing 'Bring Me Sunshine. Bring Me Love'. Only the applause was missing.

With no striding faults and only a few time faults, I reached the sanctuary of the Letterkenny Bar Room. Many of the barristers within were unfamiliar to me since they were seldom in Dublin. Those that I knew gave me a warm greeting and introduced me around.

* * *

A Circuit Bar Room is a difficult territory for a visiting barrister. Even without any mala fides on the part of your hosts, no matter how warm the welcome you are given, you are always quickly forgotten. The bewitching hour beckons. There is a List to be attended to.

The Bar Rooms tend to reflect the Courthouses themselves. Sparsely furnished, spartan. Dominated by a large table in the middle, strewn with papers and bags and dull items of clothing, a few chairs, fewer hangers, maybe a bookcase with a few dusty statutes, a phone. Off the room, a solitary toilet that you would be afraid to use for fear that every noise would be overheard. In Naas, there is a life-size portrait of a former Circuit Judge. When the Court day is done and the barristers have repaired to local pubs, the conversations and laughter linger like in an after-hours' classroom.

As you struggle with your own preparations, the pre-Court life of the Circuit goes on around you. Conversations between barristers, partly professional, partly social, with agitated solicitors trying in vain to get their attention. Not for the moment at any rate, as their barristers distribute their priority in different directions. The clients, lined up against the gable wall since 9.00 that morning, will have to wait a little longer. Eventually, of course, the barrister is free and then it's 'What is it about Donnelly? For ages fussing, trying to get you to a consultation and, of course, when you are ready, he is nowhere to be found. Solicitors!'

It is easy to be overwhelmed by the frenzied activity around you. But at least I will have one solicitor looking for my services very shortly.

★ ★ ★

Not like those never-to-be-forgotten days of my short-lived attempt to go on Circuit. Young, unknown, briefless. Briefless is the worst. No Brief to hang onto. No Solicitor. No client. Just hanging around. 'I am available for work, but I may not know what to do with it if I get it' written all over my anxious face. Surrounded by busy people in this cavernous place. Congregations of barristers and solicitors in the Bar Room. Talk of the weekend golf. A few reading the morning paper. Attaching a stud. Adjusting the wig. Looking in the bag for a Brief. A word about a case.

In the corridors outside huddle patient clients. Every nook and cranny engaged. Waiting for a moment of the busy barrister's time.

Bahamas (1973) Limited v. McGinley

Like a blessing. Before going into Court. Whispered conversations up and down the length of the labyrinthine corridors. Which I pace. Up and down. God knows how many times between 9.30 and 10.30. Like some virgin in a brothel. Without a Brief. Without anyone even to talk to. Clutching my Barrister's Notebook. Desperately trying to conceal my unemployment. To appear what I was not, namely, a barrister heading into Court to do the business. Desperate to lose my virginity. At least once the Court starts we are all equal again. Maybe I was in the previous case. Or the next. But for the moment, only the eyes of those patient clients, piercing great holes in the back of my gown as they wonder about the purpose of this young barrister's journeys from Bar Room to Courtroom and back again.

One briefless morning I arrived on Circuit, full of performance-enhancing confidence infused by Rachel the night before. Plenty of, 'Stick in there. Keep your head down. It'll come right in time. But you have to give it time. You can't expect to be in every case in the List overnight . . .' Of course, she was right and her little speech renewed my resolve.

I was only in the door of the Bar Room when one of my college contemporaries (who had shown all the courage of a castrated cat in opting for the adventure on offer in his father's solicitor's practice) greeted me with, 'Morning, McNamara. Suppose we are in everything in the List again today?' This at the top of his emasculated voice. In unison, everyone in the overcrowded Bar Room turned to witness the recipient of this early morning assassination. The strike was clinical and ruthless despite the attempt to mask it in humour. In such few words, Rachel's pep-talk of the night before was undermined. It was many hours later before an assortment of replies suggested themselves to me. For the moment, simply the hopeless resolution that if ever I were made a Judge and the self-same solicitor made the mistake of making an application in *my* Court . . .

* * *

Back to the Bar Room in Letterkenny. I still have to change my shirt. The reason for this is that Court Rules dictate that a male barrister wear a winged collar and tabs along with his wig and gown. This necessitates a collarless shirt so that one can simply swap collars. This modest degree of robing causes little problem in the Bar Room, which is essentially a sanctuary from the public for barristers and solicitors of both genders where they can engage in a little preliminary work. The Bar Room was never intended for major undressing, not even in the days before women brought their delicate delights to Circuit life. It is certainly not a place for hairy (or as the case may be, hairless) chests or protruding penes as you rush to pull your trousers up while you think no-one is looking.

Most of my colleagues, especially the older ones of the species, wore appropriate collarless shirts and encountered neither difficulty nor embarrassment in changing before an audience, whether all male or mixed. Not so I. I found the detachable collar excruciatingly uncomfortable, with studs making frontal and rear assaults on my neck, and anyway I could never do up my tie properly in the detachable collar, particularly if in a hurry, so that the entire creation disassembled as soon as it was put together.

In the event, I opted for an ordinary shirt and risked the occupational hazard of having to remove it entirely in the rare event of finding myself on Circuit in a mixed Bar Room. No matter how hard I worked at my timing, I was always at my most exhibitionist when the door of the Bar Room would open with a flourish and in would walk the three best-looking female solicitors on Circuit. It was always difficult not to feel a little compromised, a little diminished in professional stature, as you made a belated bid for your fly.

If my trip to Letterkenny had already given rise to a number of resolutions, not to have to change my shirt in the Bar Room was high on the list. So the sooner I got my gear on and got out to my consultation with Arnold and Mr. W, where I might be marginally less anonymous, the better.

* * *

Arnold was in a corner on his own, in excessive concentration on the Simplex Crossword when I greeted him. Was that a waft of alcohol and garlic that assailed my nostrils?

'Ah, Dermot. Good morning. Did you travel up last night or this morning? Where are you staying? Did you have a good night's sleep? Mr. Wilkinson will be along in a moment.'

Before I had a chance to reply to any of these enquiries, a further one was added: 'Who have we got?'

Not a very intelligent question, even for Arnold. He must have momentarily forgotten that we were on Circuit, where there was a reasonable expectation that the Circuit Judge would be sitting. As so often with Arnold, the truth is stumbled upon. Without knowing so, he had got it right. The usual incumbent wasn't sitting because of a personal involvement in a few of the cases (a throw-back to his very successful days as a practitioner on this Circuit when he was on one or other side, sometimes both, of every case).

Rogers was deputising. A popular, no-nonsense Judge, quick to make up his mind, with an inclination towards impatience. Any interruption he would make would be pertinent and would give a clear signal as to how his mind was working. Any other intervention would be along the lines, 'Have we had this before, Mr. McNamara?' If one word would suffice, there was no need for ten. He expected the same discipline from those who practised in front of him.

Rogers had not joined the Circuit Bench to contribute to the jurisprudence of the land. It was not his ambition to make the Law Reports or to have his Judgments pored over by precocious students. 'That's what those high-falutin' fellows in the High Court are paid for,' he would say. His obsession was to clear the List – and not by sitting late. 'The earlier the better' was his motto and a game of golf on the way home if at all possible.

Ronald had actually confided in me earlier that the Judge had asked him to set up a four-ball for 3.00 that afternoon – just time for nine holes before dark. (That was typical of Ronald.) It was a bit difficult to see how this might be achieved given the fact that my case was likely to last the day, in addition to which there was the usual workload for a good Circuit day. Even with Rogers' notorious reputation for speed of disposal, it was difficult to see how the List could be finished in time for golf.

In fact, if Rogers had a weakness as a Judge, it was his obsession with speed. Not that the Bar had any objection. He was great for business. But from the clients' point of view, they often left the Court less than satisfied. Rogers had a flair for getting to the truth of the case and this was borne out by the fact that he was seldom overruled on Appeal. But there was more to litigation, especially rural litigation, than getting it right. The protagonists had to have their day in Court. That was what they were paying for, after all. Sometimes with Rogers, even a winning party wasn't happy because he hadn't had a chance to sling all the mud at his disposal.

This was in marked contrast to one of Rogers' colleagues in Dublin: a losing party may still emerge content despite one of his unfavourable Judgments, satisfied that his or her case had been fully aired, over many days perhaps, with every word listened to and noted down, and every available morsel of mud well and truly launched and driven home.

We had two witnesses travelling from abroad. When this happens, it is possible to make an Application to the Court to have the case specially fixed. This has the effect of rocketing the case to No. 1 in the List, thereby guaranteeing that the case will be heard so that the witnesses coming from abroad are not unduly delayed. To my surprise, Arnold had attended to this Application.

The scene was set. Specially fixed. First in the List. Take the day. Away by 4.00. Hopefully with a win under our Bahaman belt.

'Mr. Wilkinson is anxious to get away as early as possible,' Arnold whispered to me as the éminence grise arrived. It wasn't enough apparently to win the case, but Mr. W must be away early as well. I wondered which was more important, the win or away early? More golf, I assumed. Any chance of a lift home?

I had enquired of Arnold earlier as to why Mr. W was here at all. Surely his presence was not required all the way up here, not far from the North Pole. Arnold muttered something about the importance of the case in reply. Something of a test case. First time there was a problem with this type of contract. Up to now, premiums for old rope. But obviously if the defence succeeded, all of that would change. Open the floodgates and similar clichés. Mr. W's company would end up holding the coconut, as it were. Hence Mr. W's presence. I didn't find this explanation very convincing, preferring to think that it was a few days out of town and some golf with his pal that brought him here. However, it was convincing enough to stir my adrenalin.

The consultation, when Mr. W eventually arrived, did not last very long. Arnold, with his hands-on approach, guided me through a few, largely irrelevant, areas which he felt merited consideration in front of Mr. W. To be fair to the latter, he seemed content to leave the business in my hands, though this deference may have owed more to his over-indulgence the night before than any excess of confidence in me.

Even before the consultation, I had felt that this was a case that would settle. Nothing had emerged in the course of the consultation to shake either that view or my confidence in the case. Admittedly, it would not be a popular victory. The coconuts were undoubtedly rotten and McGinley had got no value for his money. It would give no Judge satisfaction to award Judgment to a faceless foreign company against the local entrepreneur in such circumstances. But this was a Court of Law, not a Court of Sympathy, and the Law would have to be administered.

I had expected an approach from Ronald, my opponent. Indeed, I had instructions to allow a modest discount in the interests of goodwill. Surely McGinley intended to buy more coconuts? I didn't feel it was appropriate for me to make the first move. If I thought Ronald might approach me, the same thought did not seem to be exercising his mind. Notwithstanding the fact that we were first in the List, Ronald did not seem to be giving our case much attention. In fact, he didn't seem to be giving it any at all.

I have to admit that I was impressed by how busy he was. He was the sort of person who would appear busy even if he had nothing to do. But I could see that my coconuts were not his only, or even his primary, concern. He moved easily from one consultation to another, pausing in between to advance a negotiation with a colleague. From time to time, he would interrupt these travels to make or take a call on his mobile. Comparisons are odious, but no-one observing the two of us would have guessed that we came into the Library together. I was beginning to think that I had made a mistake in not coming on Circuit, trying to console myself with the knowledge that we were on his home pitch. If we were in Dublin, he would be sipping an idle coffee. Perhaps. But the sad truth is that I would probably have been sipping it with him. I envied him his command as he slipped from one client to another. I noticed how the conversation stopped immediately he rejoined a group and all eyes turned to him for the latest development or advice. In contrast, when I returned to my team, I usually had to wait until someone had finished telling a joke before receiving any attention.

Ronald and I had never quite seen eye-to-eye at College. I took my studies quite seriously and by way of extra-curricular I did some debating, which I took equally seriously. Ronald, in contrast, took nothing seriously. He was in College for a good time. His main activity was socialising and he liked to swan around Earlsfort Terrace with his jacket over his shoulders and wearing a cravat.

It was a rare event for him to grace the Archbishop Walsh Room on the first floor, and when he did it was more likely to be in pursuit of the female flavour of the month than any thirst for legal knowledge. He had an arrangement with one or two female friends who had a good attendance record and a reputation since first year for, inter alia, note-taking to make up for his absenteeism.

One could safely say that Newman's 'Idea of a University' and Ronald's bore little resemblance to one another. Ronald was unlikely to attend the lectures he should have been attending, let alone any others, and even less likely to attend a debate, Dramsoc or the English Lit. The concept of intellectual development would have startled him had it occurred to him. College was, for Ronald, a social calendar, one ball after another. He may not have debated, but that didn't stop him attending the Debating Balls. The nearest he came to preparing for life was to fill an address book. He had a wide circle of friends, most of them solicitors. Whether or not this was coincidental was a matter for conjecture. It wasn't until we hit the Library that this forward planning on Ronald's part was fully recognised. While I was busy honing my debating skills at the L&H (in the retarded belief that this might be of benefit to me in my chosen career), Ronald (far less retarded in the matter of what might or might not be of assistance to him in his career) was hosting a table at the Solicitor's Ball.

Having regard to Ronald's considerable success at the Bar in such a relatively short space of time, in spite of his total disregard of Newman's precepts, it occurred to me that the good Cardinal might usefully consider a sequel, to be called 'Alternative Idea of a University'.

Plus ça change, plus c'est la même chose. For Ronald, the Law Library, and for that matter Letterkenny Circuit Court, was an extension of Earlsfort Terrace. Different faces perhaps or maybe the same faces with new titles. Solicitors and Claims Managers to be hosted and toasted. Flitting from circle to circle outside the Courtroom in much the same way as he did a few years earlier in the Main Hall of College.

Ronald couldn't believe his luck, namely, that you could be paid for what he liked doing best – socialising.

His colleagues were not ad idem as to his ability. They did, however, agree on his mercurial success, but attributed it more to sycophantic rather than forensic skills. I had observed the former. Now for the latter.

* * *

It was now 10.30, Letterkenny-time, and no approach from Ronald. Brinkmanship, I assumed. Well, two could play at that.

'Good morning, Ladies and Gentlemen. Mr. O'Donnell, please call the List.' His Honour, Judge Rogers, Acting Judge of the North Western Circuit and part-time golfer, almost ran onto the Bench in his enthusiasm to get to grips with the List.

'Indeed, My Lord. *Bahamas (1973) Limited v. McGinley*, Specially Fixed', announces the Registrar.

I rose to my visiting feet. 'Going on, My Lord.'

'How long will it take, Mr. Eh?'

'McNamara, My Lord. The day, I think, My Lord.'

The Registrar turned around and had a muted conversation with His Lordship. I had a certain foreboding.

'Did your solicitor inform the Registrar that the case was likely to take the day, Mr. McNamara?'

'If I may take instructions, My Lord?' Arnold mustn't have heard the Judge's enquiry because I had to repeat it to him. In a less than muted conversation, Arnold gave me a long-winded explanation for why he didn't inform the Registrar. His Lordship would not be very interested in the why not.

'Well, Mr. McNamara?' asks the Judge impatiently.

'It appears not, My Lord.'

'Mr. O'Donnell informs me that it is the practice on his Circuit to inform the Registrar if the case is likely to take more than half a day. It is not your fault, of course, Mr. McNamara. It is a matter for your solicitor.' Arnold could hear everything now. In sporting parlance, he was focused. 'It is an unfortunate aspect of practitioners crossing Circuits and places an even-greater onus on the visiting solicitor to make all necessary enquiries as to the local rules,' continued

His Lordship. He seemed to have forgotten momentarily his own visitor's status. 'What am I to do, Mr. McNamara?'

'Well, My Lord, I apologise for the fact that the Registrar was not adequately informed, but my solicitor instructs me that we have two witnesses from abroad and we would be most anxious to have the case heard.'

'That's all very well, Mr. McNamara, but you tell me that this case will take the day. There is a full List for hearing today and each day this week, and if your case goes on it will cause considerable inconvenience to a great number of innocent people. A simple communication from your solicitor and this problem would not have arisen. I simply can't start the case now. Who's for the Defendant?'

'I am, My Lord,' announces Ronald, breaking his tactful silence. 'Perhaps if Your Lordship were to let the matter stand for the moment. In the meantime, Mr. McNamara and I will use our best endeavours to dispose of the case amicably and thereby save the Court's valuable time. In fact, I have already had a word with Mr. McNamara and given a little time we may be able to resolve matters. I gather Your Lordship has to rise early, so that if we don't settle, Your Lordship can decide what to do with the case at that stage.'

A consummate display of forensic skill by Ronald, I had to admit. In a few short sentences, he had managed to get the case put back, which suited him and his colleagues and the Judge. They could all now get on with the remainder of the List and, with the exception of the Judge, make some money. He had given the Judge the impression that he had initiated settlement discussions and that my Client was the difficult one. He had also announced that the Judge would have to rise early, thereby saving His Lordship any embarrassment in relation to his extra-curricular appointment.

The Judge seemed well-pleased with this advice from one so young. 'Very well then. Two o'clock. Liberty to mention the case at two o'clock.'

Arnold was furious. 'Doesn't the Judge realise I have come all the way from Dublin?' He did. (As if this was some great favour bestowed on Letterkenny by Arnold.) 'Doesn't the Judge realise that we have two witnesses from abroad?' He did. 'Does the Judge think that I can spend the whole week in Letterkenny?' The Judge hadn't give it a thought one way or the other.

Bahamas (1973) Limited v. McGinley

'Why didn't you insist the case go on, Dermot? After all, it was specially fixed. What more could I have done?' pleaded Arnold, embarrassed in front of Mr. Wilkinson by this development.

'You could have informed the Registrar that the case would take the day, like the Judge said. Were you not listening?' I replied inaudibly. My audible explanation did not satisfy Arnold either.

While this exchange was in full flight, Mr. W slipped off to the leisure centre in his hotel where he hoped to tame the excesses of the previous night. Arnold was not far behind.

* * *

I had long since abandoned as unworthy my early suspicion that Ronald had tried to sabotage my trip to Letterkenny. Now I began to realise that more subtle influences were at work. Playing away from home. Local rules apply. The smooth working of the Sessions was not going to be upset by the machinations of a Dublin solicitor specially fixing a long case for the first day. Maybe Mr. W was right after all. Maybe Bahamas 1973 would have been better served by an on-course solicitor and barrister. For the first time since 4.00 on the previous Friday afternoon, a seed of self-doubt was sown. Perhaps the result was not the foregone conclusion I had thought. The local businessman might have a friend in Court.

I knew now why Ronald had not paid me any attention before the Court sat. He knew, as I did not, that there was no chance of Rogers taking our case first and, accordingly, he could devote himself to his other cases. God knows when we would now be heard and neither God nor Ronald cared. There was nothing for it but to hang around until two o'clock.

I had ample opportunity to observe His Lordship. His reputation for speed was well-founded. He heard cases in the time it took other Judges to call over the List. He got through more work on that Monday morning than many of his colleagues would achieve in a week. Not without casualties, of course. The barrister who felt that some of the evidence might bear repeating: 'I think we have had this before, Mr. Sweeney.' Or the Defendant who regarded every question as his cue for a speech: 'If you could confine your evidence to the question, Mr. Boyce, and leave the speeches to the politicians.'

Judge Rogers did not see it as any part of his function to provide a forum for the airing of grievances. His job was to administer justice, to hear such evidence as it was necessary for him to hear for the purpose of getting to the truth of the matter as he saw it, and to make a decision accordingly. For this reason, witnesses would be interrupted, even eliminated. A case might be cut short long before its natural conclusion because the Judge had made up his mind. It was the job of the barristers to net the case down to its bare essentials.

Rogers was consistent. He didn't permit elaboration from those who appeared in front of him and he didn't go in for it himself. His interventions were not numerous, but they were exacting. You ignored them at your peril. His Judgments were more in the form of decisions than judicial tracts. He found either for the Plaintiff or the Defendant and very often did not say much more. He gave the impression that deciding came easily to him. Sometimes this was a little frustrating, both for Counsel and client. Sometimes one wished to know which particular witness had impressed His Lordship, which particular piece of evidence had exercised his mind, but the student of the judicial process, looking for a unique insight into the workings of the judicial mind, would as likely as not be disappointed. It was not the ambition of this Judge to have his Judgments pondered by posterity.

Ronald, too, was on view and not to any disadvantage. He had made some guineas by 2.00pm. There were still a few senior to him on the Circuit, but he was head and shoulders above his contemporaries. There was no evidence that his around-the-clock service to solicitors was anything but a major success. One of the local solicitors may have joked that he had to check his filing cabinet every evening before closing his office to make sure Ronald wasn't in it, drumming up another file, but it didn't stop him sending the entire of his practice to him.

It doesn't come easily to say it, but he was competent on his feet. I had always thought him something of a featherweight in College, but it appeared from his Court performance this Monday morning that his solicitor-friendly, out-of-Court manner was backed up by a certain adroitness in Court.

The colleague who depends for his Briefs on the social attentions he gives his solicitor is hard enough to take. But at least if he is awful in Court, this affords some satisfaction and further grounds for character assassination. If, on the other hand, he is good at his job, then one's attack is seriously undermined by the grudging respect one has to pay to his ability.

Ronald wins on both counts. He is better than you at garnering the work and, once garnered, better than you at executing it. Irritating in much the same way as the loser on merit might prefer to be beaten by the offspring of the managing director. Ronald fell into this category, namely, he danced attention on his solicitors, but he could also deliver the goods.

Ronald and the Judge were very comfortable with each other. Once or twice during the morning, the Judge had to interrupt Counsel, but not Ronald. Not surprising, you might say, seeing that they had a rendezvous for golf. But I think it was more than that. Ronald was able to read Rogers well. He knew when to pursue something and when to stop.

As for the golf, the arrangement for the afternoon sprang from their acquaintance with one another through the Bar Golf Society. It was not often that one not yet of any seniority at the Bar would be socialising with a Circuit Judge. But that was one of the benefits of the Golf Society. It was typical of Ronald to enlist early on in his career. Too obvious an opportunity to be overlooked. And here it was paying dividends at an early stage. I had better be careful or Ronald will be travelling home with Arnold and Mr. W, eighteen holes on the way.

* * *

Miraculously, by 2.00pm, the List had cleared and *Bahamas (1973) Limited v. McGinley* was called for the second time.

'Well, Mr. Browning, have you been able to resolve your differences?' enquired His Lordship, addressing Ronald, even though I was for the Plaintiff – eloquent testimony as to how dominant Ronald had been during the morning and how well he got on with the Judge.

'Unfortunately not, My Lord,' replied Ronald, without adding that he had not even approached me in the interim.

'In that case, do you think that we will finish this afternoon?'

'That really depends on how long my friend will be, My Lord. I will only have one witness who I anticipate will be short, that is if I have to call him,' replied Ronald, passing the buck very neatly.

'Well, Mr. Eh?' enquired the Judge, fixing his attention on me.

'McNamara, My Lord. I doubt it, My Lord. I have two witnesses and I think they will take a little time,' I offered.

'This is most unsatisfactory. What I will do is I will start the case and as I have to rise at 3.00 due to a prior commitment, I will resume the case at the end of tomorrow's List. Does that suit the parties?'

It may have suited the Judge and Ronald and his client and every other practitioner and party in Letterkenny that week. But it most certainly did not suit Arnold, some of whose disappointment, expressed sotto voce in part, must have reached His Lordship on the Bench. Arnold was urging me to mention again our two witnesses from abroad and to throw in Mr. W's predicament for good measure, not omitting Arnold's practice in Dublin.

'As your Lordship pleases' was the best effort I could make to convey all of Arnold's messages, altering the inflection with each word as appropriate in an attempt to capture the precise mood of the members of our team. As for myself, all I could think of was how I was going to afford the hotel for the rest of the week. There weren't enough words or inflections to cover that concern.

'The sooner we start, the sooner we finish,' pronounced His Lordship.

* * *

With some Judges, it was a good idea to open at some length because they took a note of Counsel's opening and then had a tendency to treat that as the evidence, so that even if the witness did not come up to scratch, the opening merged with the evidence and became fact in the learned Judge's mind. Learning from what I had observed during the morning, I decided to open the case briefly. But not briefly enough for Rogers.

'Mr. McNamara! I have read the papers. Perhaps we might get on with the evidence.' (Precisely what I wanted to avoid, not getting on with the evidence, but having to be prompted by the Judge . . .)

'Come up, Mr. Nicholls.'

Bahamas (1973) Limited v. McGinley

Gordon Nicholls was one of two witnesses for the Plaintiff. Born in the south of England, he was a graduate of the London School of Economics. He ran a number of companies before finally settling down with Bahamas (1973) Limited as MD, seven years previously. He lived in Panama. It was a measure of the importance Mr. Wilkinson attached to this case that Mr. Nicholls had travelled all the way from Panama to Letterkenny for the hearing. A measure also of the importance of Mr. Nicholls and Mr. Wilkinson, one to another. After all, Mr. Nicholls' evidence (little more than the ordering of the coconuts and their safe delivery) could have been given by the company accountant or book-keeper and certainly by the person who dealt with Mr. McGinley. But Mr. Wilkinson wanted nothing left to chance and it was his suggestion that the MD himself might travel.

Nicholls was not very far into his evidence and was in the process of arranging a countless number of order forms and invoices on the bench in front of him when Judge Rogers interrupted.

'Mr. Browning, I presume that none of this is in issue. You are not denying that you ordered and received the coconuts or are you?'

'No, My Lord, we accept that we ordered and received the coconuts,' Ronald replied agreeably.

'In fact, all of this could have been agreed in correspondence before the trial or by a Notice to Admit Facts?'

'Quite so, My Lord. In fact, we have never denied any of this. We have always made it quite plain what our grievance was.'

'My friend is not quite correct in this, My Lord.' I interjected. 'The Contract is denied in the Defence.'

'That may be so, Mr. McNamara, but we all know that pleadings rarely tell us very much about what the case is really about. All your solicitor had to do was to take up the phone to Mr. Browning's solicitor and all of this could have been ironed out and Mr. Nicholls' journey from Panama could have been avoided and he could be working on his next coconut, so to speak, instead of wasting his time in Letterkenny.'

I could sense Arnold's rage, but what could I say? Wasn't the Judge right?

'I take it, Mr. Browning, that the real issue in this case, the core of the case if I may put it that way, is whether or not the coconuts were damaged and, if they were, who bears the responsibility, seller or purchaser? Is that right?'

'That's it in a nutshell, if your Lordship will excuse the pun,' quipped Ronald.

A smile from His Lordship. I was beginning to find this cosy relationship a bit irritating. Particularly as I sensed that there was no room in it for me. The more the case progressed, the more of an outsider I was made to feel. The Circuit could look after its own without any resort to ostracism and even, it appeared, with a visiting Judge.

'Well, Mr. McNamara, back to you. I don't think we need to trouble Mr. Nicholls any longer.' I ushered a puzzled-looking Mr. Nicholls from the witness box. 'Is that your case, Mr. McNamara?'

In fact, His Lordship was right. That was my case. I had established my entitlement to be paid for my coconuts. It was up to the Defendant now to say why he should not pay. However, from the pleadings, I knew what the defence was and I wanted to deal with this.

'No, My Lord. One more witness. Dr. Benson, please.'

★ ★ ★

George Benson was an impeccably dressed black American. Tall and of athletic build, he cut an impressive figure in the Courthouse of Letterkenny. He was our star witness and as he made his authoritative way to the witness box, he gave the distinct impression of being someone not to be trifled with.

I thought I should bring him through his qualifications. 'Dr. Benson, you reside and work in Paris?' 'That is correct, Mr. McNamara.' 'You are an arbitrator by profession, specialising in coconut contracts, and you conduct these arbitrations in Paris mostly, but also at venues around the world and have done so for upwards of twenty years?' 'That is correct.' 'Please tell His Lordship of your qualifications.' Dr. Benson took the Judge through each of his qualifications with great deliberation, savouring each as one might a good wine.

'My Lord, I went to private school in the United States, after which I obtained a scholarship for Law School in Harvard University. I graduated with a first-class honours degree. After that, I did a Master's in Contract Law, specialising in international contracts. By that time, I had become interested in the arbitration process. I did a doctorate in the enforcement of fruit contracts and then became qualified as an international arbitrator. Paris is one of the international centres for arbitration and so I studied French and have lived and worked in Paris for the last twenty years.'

At last, I began to feel that our case was on a firm footing. Up to now, it looked as if Rogers might rail-road the case and not give it a proper hearing. But Dr. Benson had steadied matters. For one, Judge Rogers and Dr. Benson were equals, or almost so, in that both were judicial or quasi-judicial figures. In addition, Dr. Benson brought to the hearing in Letterkenny an international dimension. Judge Rogers would not want it whispered around judicial circles in Paris that banana justice was being dispensed by him in this Celtic outpost of Europe. There was no way Dr. Benson's evidence could be agreed over the phone.

'Tell His Lordship about your work as an international arbitrator specialising in coconut contracts.'

'Certainly. The coconut industry is a multi-million pound industry . . . (this was a little more exotic than the usual February fare in Letterkenny Courthouse) . . . The dealers attend the coconut markets at several venues around the world. A number of these are located in the Caribbean . . . (images of silken sand and coral sea, grass skirt and distant drum) . . . These dealers act on behalf of suppliers, most of whom operate out of London, Paris and New York. Bahamas (1973) Limited is exceptional in that it is based in Panama. Suppliers such as Bahamas sell on to agents like Mr. McGinley who serve the home markets.'

His Lordship was fidgeting with his pencil.

'Where does arbitration come into it, Dr. Benson?' I asked.

'Well, disputes arise from time to time. More often than not, these relate to non-payment of money or delay in delivery or dissatisfaction with the goods. The buying and selling is governed by internationally agreed contracts which provide for resolution of disputes by arbitration. This circumvents Court delays and long drawn-out arguments about jurisdiction. Over the years, a sophisticated arbitration network has grown up to service the coconut industry. If, for some reason, the dispute cannot come to Paris or other recognized arbitration centre, the arbitration can move easily and quickly to the location of the dispute.'

His Lordship intervened. 'Mr. McNamara, what Dr. Benson has to say is fascinating and were more time available, I can think of no more charming way of passing a dreary day in Donegal than listening to his articulate account of his exciting life. But I fear time is not on our side and I wonder if you could direct his evidence to the real issues in the case?'

'Of course, My Lord.' One of the difficulties I was having with my witness was that while a formidable witness, he had a tendency to be less than succinct in his responses. I would have to see what I could do.

'Dr. Benson, you have heard His Lordship say how helpful he found your outline of the background to this case. Could we now perhaps come on to the specific question of responsibility in the situation where the coconuts are defective. Can you assist the Court from your vast experience as to the position there?'

'Indeed I can, Mr. McNamara. But before coming to that, it is important that His Lordship, who may not be familiar with the ins and outs of the coconut industry, should know . . . (Oh no, Dr. Benson, please don't patronize His Lordship) . . . that the coconut is a sensitive fruit, vulnerable to many different types of disease. The most common ailment is coconut-weevil, a sort of coconut acne brought about by the predatory activity of adult weevils feeding on the young coconut, which unfortunately does not manifest itself until the coconut is comfortably settled in the home of the intending consumer. If he is lucky, he will simply have a bad coconut which he will return to his greengrocer. If unlucky, he will have consumed it and the après-consumption is a rather grim business, lasting several days, invariably culminating in litigation. The domino effect goes back up the line until, as in this case, Bahamas (1973) Limited has to sue the agent, Mr. McGinley, for its money.'

'Yes, Dr. Benson. But what His Lordship wants to know is who is responsible?'

'I am coming to that, but there is one more vital piece of information and it is the role of insurance. Because of the vulnerable disposition of the coconut, anyone coming remotely near a coconut contract protects himself with insurance cover, which is readily available at a modest premium.'

'Responsibility, Dr. Benson?'

'The buyer.'

'Thank you, Dr. Benson. Is that in all cases?' 'Almost all.' 'What was your diagnosis in relation to these coconuts?' 'The very coconut-weevil that I have been talking about.' 'And your expert evidence is, Dr. Benson, that if the coconuts are suffering from weevil the buyer bears the loss?' 'That is correct.'

An interruption from the impatient Bench. 'Did you see these coconuts, Dr. Benson?'

'I am afraid not, My Lord. They were well and truly destroyed by the time I was engaged.' Rogers nods quizzically in the direction of Ronald and then takes a deliberate note, his first.

I continued, 'And your evidence is, Dr. Benson, that to protect himself against the volatile condition of the coconut, the buyer simply arranges insurance?' 'Precisely.' 'And was there insurance in this case?'

'Mr. McNamara!' interrupts His Lordship, 'As you well know, I should not be told of the existence or not of insurance cover. I must decide this case on the facts and whether or not a party was insured does not come into it.'

'Of course, My Lord.'

And on that low note, I resumed my seat with an uneasy feeling that unseen forces were at work.

* * *

Ronald rose to his small, but effective feet. 'Dr. Benson, you have very fairly told His Lordship that you did not examine the coconuts in question. Isn't that so?' 'It is.' 'How can you purport to give an expert opinion in relation to the damage to these coconuts without having seen them?' 'I saw photographs.' 'You saw photographs?' 'Yes.' 'And is it on the basis of these photographs that you came to the conclusion that these coconuts were suffering from coconut-weevil?' 'Yes.' 'And may I see these photographs?'

Dr. Benson looked a little uncomfortable.

'I take it that I cannot. Why is it that they are not available?' 'I left them in my hotel room. I didn't think they would be required.' 'You didn't think that they would be required? I see. Is it possible to identify the ailment simply on the basis of photographs?' 'More or less.' 'What do you mean "more or less"?' 'Well in ninety per cent of cases, the damage is this coconut-weevil.' 'That is exactly what I was coming to, Dr. Benson. Isn't it the position that there is another similar condition that has an artificial rather than a natural cause?' 'It is.' 'Well, Dr. Benson, tell His Lordship about this condition, that accounts for ten per cent of the damaged cases.'

'My Lord, in the past it was the practice of coconut-farmers to inject their coconuts with a hormone that enhanced growth. More recently, it was discovered that this treatment gave rise to certain undesirable side-effects with the result that this treatment was proscribed by law. Sometimes where this treatment was administered, the coconuts themselves would become affected in a manner similar to the more common coconut-weevil. Now the practice is that the coconut-farmers give an undertaking that their crop has not received this treatment.'

'And if the farmer breaches that undertaking, so that the coconuts become damaged from the treatment, the seller bears the loss, isn't that right?' 'Yes.'

News to me. And to Arnold, who is in mayday communication with Mr. Wilkinson at the back of the Court. Rogers wants to know why Dr. Benson didn't deal with this in his direct evidence, to which he makes the inadequate, but no-less-often-used reply, 'I wasn't asked'.

'To distinguish between coconut-weevil on the one hand and the condition that results from performance-enhancing hormone treatment on the other requires a meticulous examination of the actual coconuts, isn't that so?' 'Yes.' 'You couldn't reliably identify whether it was one or the other on the basis of photographs, could you?' 'No.' 'And, in fact, that would be for a coconut surgeon, rather than an arbitrator?' 'Yes, if there is an issue as to which type the damage is in this case, a coconut surgeon would be required.' 'In summary, Dr. Benson, you cannot rule out the possibility that Mr. McGinley's coconuts received this treatment?' 'I think it unlikely in the extreme, but since you put it like that, no, I cannot.'

I didn't like the direction the case was taking. Arnold seemed to be a bit put out also, judging by the increase in the number of missiles being passed my way. Ronald, apparently, had not finished.

'Dr. Benson, let us assume for a moment that the disease contracted by this batch of coconuts was the coconut-weevil contended by you. How was Mr. McGinley to know that if the coconuts came down with this condition that he would bear the loss and have no redress against the supplier?'

'Quite simply, Mr. Browning, it is inconceivable that anyone could enter this market without knowing. It is part of the ABC of the business. The birds in the air know it, so to speak. One couldn't be five minutes in the marketplace without knowing.'

'That is all very well for you to say, Dr. Benson, with your easy familiarity borne of years of experience with the coconut marketplace and its ways and means. However, would anyone have informed Mr. McGinley formally, as it were, of this fact?'

'I think that it is so well known that no-one would have actually informed him of it.'

'Well, would it have been included in the contract? Would it have been written down anywhere so that he could read it? For example, in the order form?'

'I don't think so. Again, I think it is so well known that he would have picked it up.'

Rogers again, incredulously, 'Picked it up, Dr. Benson? You would have expected Mr. McGinley to pick it up?'

'Yes, My Lord.'

'Such a vital term that, in this instance, obliges the Defendant to bear the loss of £20,000 worth of coconuts would not be written down and made a contractual term, but the Defendant would be expected to pick it up?'

'Yes, My Lord. This might seem a little strange in the rarefied atmosphere of Your Lordship's Court, but I can assure you that if Your Lordship were to visit the marketplace you would readily understand what I am saying.' Rogers was not listening to this apologia, but instead was recording his second note of the proceedings.

Back to Ronald. 'If I tell you that Mr. McGinley was dealing in this market for the first time, is it reasonable to suggest that he might not have been aware of this feature of the transaction?'

'Not unless he was going around with his ears tightly closed.'

'If he was, as it were, a virgin in this foreign field, might he not be unaware of this draconian liability?'

'Once again, I think that it is unlikely, but if you phrase it like that, I have to answer that he might be.'

'Thank you, Dr. Benson.'

Ronald resumed his seat, a little smugly. I have to accept that he had played well, albeit with the wind behind him. Dr. Benson made his way from the witness box back to his place in the body of the Court.

* * *

'Could Mr. Nicholls come back, please?' the Judge said.

'Certainly, My Lord.'

'Mr. Nicholls, you are already sworn. You have heard Dr. Benson's evidence. I wonder if you can assist the Court? By any chance, did you see these coconuts? After all, you were the person immediately involved?'

'I am afraid not, My Lord. I couldn't possibly inspect every coconut contract individually.'

'I see. Thank you, Mr. Nicholls. You may go down.'

I thought it would be a good idea to ask the Judge to release my two witnesses so that they could make their way back to Dublin and away to their international destinations and not delay them in Letterkenny while the case continued. I didn't have time to make this Application, however.

Ronald was back on his feet, but not to call Mr. McGinley. Instead, 'My Lord, I have an Application to make.'

'Yes, Mr. Browning?'

I couldn't believe my ears. This wasn't a case for a direction. At the very least, the Defendant would have to go into evidence.

'It is common case that these coconuts were flawed. Prima facie, my client shouldn't have to pay for them. It is up to the Plaintiff to satisfy Your Lordship that the flaws were such that the loss was transferred from Plaintiff to Defendant. Neither Dr. Benson nor Mr. Nicholls saw the coconuts. Therefore, the Plaintiff cannot satisfy Your Lordship that the condition of the coconuts was due to weevil. It may just as well have been due to the illegal hormone treatment, in which case the Plaintiff bears the loss. It is up to the Plaintiff to prove his case. In the light of the evidence of Dr. Benson and Mr. Nicholls, I submit that I should not be required to go into evidence.'

'I agree, Mr. Browning.'

'Dismiss, My Lord?'

'Dismiss, Mr. Browning.'

'Costs, My Lord?'

'Costs, Mr. Browning.'

'Golf, My Lord?' I thought I heard, but perhaps not.

'My Lord,' I stuttered, 'I would like an opportunity to reply to my friend's unmeritorious Application.'

'Very well, Mr. McNamara, though really I have made my decision.'

I set out my thoughts as to how the Defendant ought to be required to give evidence and that a prima facie case had been made out and that until Mr. McGinley had given evidence that the coconuts were flawed because of the treatment they had got, and further that he was not aware of the term that he was responsible for coconut-weevil, His Lordship was obliged to find for the Plaintiff.

His Lordship wasn't listening. Far less did he feel obliged to find in accordance with my recommendations.

'Is that all, Mr. McNamara? I don't wish to cut you short.'

In a flash of inspiration, I recognized the futility of what I was doing and sat down.

Judge Rogers delivered himself of one of his legendary Judgments: 'Mr. McNamara – all the way from Dublin – excellent job – did everything he could – only as good as his tools – Dr. Benson very impressive – under handicap – didn't see the coconuts – dangerous to convict (Rogers was obviously forgetting that this was a civil case and there was no question of convicting anyone) – McGinley, a virgin – out of his depth – innocent abroad – Dismiss – Costs.'

Golf.

Flabbergasted. Gobsmacked. My watertight coconut case.

As Judge Rogers finished his Judgment, I looked up at the clock. One minute to three.

'Is there anything left in the List, Mr. O'Donnell?' 'No, My Lord.' 'Very well, 10.30 tomorrow morning.'

As I left the Courtroom, I heard Ronald modestly explaining how you win some, you lose some. All in all, a stunning home win. Against all the odds. Well, most of them anyway.

I joined a less-than-euphoric Arnold and Mr. W. 'Smart young lad, your colleague Browning,' commented Mr. W. What could I say? It didn't seem prudent to mention home advantage. Mr. W had his back to the Judge's chambers and therefore didn't see Rogers slip out, barely concealing his golf bag, and into the silver BMW, where Ronald was already waiting to transport them off for a few holes before dark.

I didn't expect to be offered a lift home. And the offer was not forthcoming. I settled for the bus, tomorrow another day.

★ ★ ★

Words and Phrases

Application for a direction: Absolutely nothing to do with losing one's way in the Four Courts. If, at the end of the Plaintiff's evidence, his or her case looks very weak, Defence Counsel will 'apply for a direction', i.e. will ask the Judge to throw the case out, without the necessity for the Defendant to go into the witness box.

Archbishop Walsh Room: Aficionados of UCD, when it was located in Earlsfort Terrace, will recall attending (or not, as the case may be) Law and other lectures in this room, dedicated to the memory of William Walsh, Archbishop of Dublin during the years 1885-1921.

Bar: (*depending on the context*) A comparatively long and generally massive rod or strip of any solid substance; a licensed premises; barristers or advocates collectively.

Bench: A long seat (if it has a little 'b'); otherwise (with a big 'b'), the body or assembly of Judges.

Benchers: Senior members of the Bar and Bench who are responsible for the education of barristers and the running of the King's Inns.

The Bridewell: The name given to the District Courts behind the Four Courts and beside The Bridewell Garda Station, where many a criminal *cause célèbre* begins.

Brief: A bundle of papers, not in any particular order, formerly bound in a pink ribbon, which purports to contain all the information a barrister needs for the proper running of the case, but is unlikely to.

Call-over of the List: At the crack of dawn (10.30 approximately), the Judge calls over the List of cases to be heard in that Court on that day, for the purpose of ascertaining which cases have settled and which have not and, in relation to the latter, how long they will take; at this point, there would appear to be a term's work in the day's List, but somehow, it is not clear how, by long day's end (4 o'clock approximately), the List is cleared.

Circuit Dinner: The country is divided into Circuits; each Circuit has its own Judge or Judges who wander around the Circuit dispensing Justice; barristers who choose to go on Circuit, rather than practise exclusively in Dublin, join a Circuit; from time to time, the Circuit holds a dinner, usually a most sober and celibate occasion that anyone with anything remotely better to do will be anxious to avoid.

Consultation room: The room in which the consultation, between Barrister, Solicitor, Client and Witnesses, is held before going into Court. Usually a poky, over-heated, under-ventilated, subterranean chamber, an essential feature of which is that the entire, highly confidential, proceedings can be overheard in the adjoining room, more than likely occupied by the other side.

The Court below: Nothing to do with the Court on the floor below. An hierarchical reference to the Court from which an appeal is brought.

De bene esse: The dictionary says, 'To take evidence for future use while it is available'. In practice, what happens is that the Judge has not the faintest idea of whether or not certain evidence is admissible and so he receives it '*de bene esse*'. Everyone is happy: the Judge because he has resolved the altercation; Counsel for the Plaintiff because the Judge has heard the controversial evidence; Counsel for the Defendant because the Judge may yet direct himself to banish the evidence from his mind.

Devilling: Every barrister is obliged to make a nuisance of himself in his first year; he or she works with an established barrister and hopefully learns the trade. In less exalted circles, this term would be known as an apprenticeship.

Dinners in the King's Inns: A sort of mandatory meals-on-wheels for student barristers, one of the purposes of which is to instil sociability among colleagues; in bygone halcyon days, aspiring barristers sat dinners, not exams.

Earlsfort Terrace: An artery leading from St. Stephen's Green to Rathmines and other salubrious suburbs; when its most famous feature was in danger of being razed to the ground during The Gentle Revolution of 1969, UCD was soon after banished to the new university campus of Belfield and replaced in Earlsfort Terrace by the National Concert Hall.

Four Courts: You really can't miss it – a pre-1963 edifice (planning permission not required) standing on the northern bank of Dublin's River Liffey, halfway between O'Connell Bridge and Heuston Station, in a designated area (double rent allowance) and designed by a gentleman named Mr. Gandon.

Hospital pass: When a colleague purports to do a junior colleague a favour; for example, 'Are you free to do a building contract case tomorrow?'

Junior on the Circuit: The most recent recruit to the Circuit, on whose shoulders fall many arduous duties such as organising the Circuit Dinner.

King's Inns: The Honorable Society of King's Inns – another one of Mr. Gandon's buildings, the foundation stone of which was laid in 1800 – casts a cold eye on Henrietta Street and on the education of aspiring barristers.

L&H: Literary and Historical Society, a debating society in UCD, second only in importance to the Law Society.

Law Library: The engine room of the Four Courts, its nerve centre, as it were, from where the vast majority of the country's barristers ply their trade in conditions of total confidentiality; otherwise, a place where love stories begin, gallons of coffee are consumed and, occasionally, some work is done (though my daughter insists that there is little evidence of this from her visits).

Long Vacation: That portion of the summer (most of it) when the Courts and Law Library are closed.

A mark: Whether or not the Plaintiff/Defendant has assets – an important factor in the assessment of whether or not to bring a highly speculative action.

Master: The senior party to the Master/Devil relationship. For one glorious year, the Master receives the unqualified respect of his Devil, who looks on him as a sort of god until, as the years unfold, the Devil discovers that the Master was not quite the legal luminary he cracked himself up to be.

'On the taxi rank': Barristers, like taxis, are for hire.

Robing Room: Place where barristers dress up. Also, according to one distinguished source, the place where Briefs, with or without pink ribbons, are handed over.

Round Hall: The centre of High Court litigation, situated in Dublin's Four Courts. More than likely, so called for its shape; could equally have been called the Rotunda, though this might have been confusing for expectant mothers.

Running-down cases: Legalese for motor accident cases.

Senior Counsel (SC): Practising barristers come in two categories: Junior Counsel and Senior Counsel. In the main, the former practise in the District and Circuit Courts, and have mountains of paperwork, while the latter are to be found in the High and Supreme Courts, and have considerably less paperwork. Other minor differences are that Senior Counsel work a four-day week for 50% higher fees.

Statute-barred: It's too late! Don't waste your time taking a case.

Take Silk: What Junior Counsel does when he or she wishes to progress to a four-day week for higher fees, namely, applies to the Government for a 'Grant of Letters Patent' which, if granted, will be presented at a ceremony in the Supreme Court when he or she is called to the Inner Bar, with the right thereafter to wear a silk gown.

Tommy: Mr. Thomas Whelan, Crier, who fronted the Law Library for many years. He joined the staff of the Library in 1930, at the age of 14, and retired in 1988. A gentleman and the first friend every barrister made upon arrival in the Library.